Do you like
dragons, wizards,
and talking lizards?

Geronimo Stilton

THE DRAGON OF FORTUNE

AN EPIC KINGDOM OF FANTASY ADVENTURE

Scholastic Inc.

Library of Congress Cataloging-in-Publication Data available

ISBN 978-1-338-15939-4

Text by Geronimo Stilton
Original title *Grande ritorno nel Regno della Fantasia 2*
Cover by Silvia Fusetti
Illustrations by Silvia Bigolin, Federico Brusco, Carla Debernardi, Alessandro Muscillo, and Piemme's Archives. Color by Christian Aliprandi
Graphics by Marta Lorini and Daria Colombo

Special thanks to Kathryn Cristaldi
Translated by Julia Heim
Interior design by Kay Petronio

10 9 8 7 6 5 4   19 20 21 22

Printed in China   62

First edition, September 2017

Psst . . . It's me,
Geronimo Stilton
in the fur!
Get ready, I'm returning
to the magical
Kingdom of Fantasy!

A THOUSAND
SILVER VIOLINS

It all started one spring at the **crack** of dawn. I was having a dream. No, scratch that. I was having a **NIGHTMARE**!

I tossed and turned, and tossed and turned, and tossed and turned . . .

In my dream a familiar face hovered over me. Was it **Blossom**, the sweet **Queen of the Fairies**? It sure looked like her, but when I

Humph . . .

peered closer a **shiver** ran down my fur. It wasn't Blossom at all. It was Wither, Blossom's evil twin sister!

She was surrounded by strange flying creatures. They looked like witches with wings. In fact, they were . . .

THE DARK FAIRIES!

The dark fairies grabbed their *silver violins* and began to play. Unfortunately, it wasn't happy dance music (you know, the kind that makes you want to kick up your paws). This melody was disturbing.

Next the fairies began to sing.

OF THIS WE WARN . . . THE TIME IS RIGHT . . .

THE VEIL IS TORN . . . ENTER THE NIGHT!

What did that mean? It couldn't be good. The dark fairies are not known for their kindhearted nature.

I woke up squeaking. Then I jumped out of bed so fast I jumped right out of my pajamas. Well, okay, I didn't *really* jump out of my pj's, but you get the idea. WHAT A NIGHTMARE!

What a nightmare!

ENTER THE NIGHT!
Heh, heh, heh!
OF THIS WE WARN . . .
THE TIME IS RIGHT . . .
THE VEIL IS TORN . . .
ENTER THE NIGHT!

I rubbed my eyes trying to **erase** the image of those dark fairies. I had met them during one of my recent trips to the Kingdom of Fantasy. On that trip, Wither had ordered the fairies to **imprison** her sister.

Luckily, not to brag or anything, I saved the day! That's right, I rescued Blossom! As a reward, the queen named me *Prince Fearless, Prince of the Winged Ones*. She also gave me a pair of cool *blue wings* and a blue winged ring. The

ring had special powers. It allowed me to travel to and from the Kingdom of Fantasy.

Just thinking about my fantastic adventures made me smile. Don't get me wrong, these trips were never easy. They were filled with dangerous treks, **WICKED SPELLS**, and horrifying creatures. But the friends I made in the Kingdom of Fantasy were worth it!

Winged Ring

The dark fairies imprisoned Blossom . . .

. . . but I rescued her!

Thank you for saving me, Knight!

As a reward, the queen gave me the Winged Ring!

Right then I noticed the clock on my nightstand. Rats! I was **late** for work!

I threw on my clothes and raced outside.

It was the first day of *spring*, and I expected to see the sun shining, flowers blooming, and birds singing in a blue sky. Instead . . .

There was a **freezing** northern wind . . . The sky was filled with GRAY CLOUDS . . .

And the only birds were black crows shrieking, **"Caw! Caw! Caw! Caw!"**

You couldn't smell the sweet scent of flowers.
Instead there was the disgusting scent of sulfur!

THE THICK

GRAY CLOUDS

MADE IT HARD

TO SEE...

What is the shape in the sky?

Answers on page 572

It was a

strange,

no,

the strangest,

no,

the super-strangest

spring morning!

FLAP! FLAP! FLAP!

Still, what could I do? I had to get to the office. So I grabbed a coat and scarf and left.

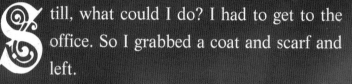

Brrr, it was so cold my whiskers froze!

Answers on page 572

As I raced down that FOGGY street, I noticed something else that was strange.

All the rodents I passed had DARK CIRCLES under their eyes. They looked like they hadn't slept a wink.

"Good morning!" I called to **BOBBY BABBLESNOUT**, the mouse who ran the newsstand. "How are you?"

"Exhausted," Bobby mumbled with eyes half-closed. "For some reason I was up tossing and turning all night long."

What is the shape in the sky?

What is
the shape in
the sky?

Next, I passed the florist, MISS GARDENIA. She had bags under her eyes, too, and she was **YAWNING** up a storm. How strange.

Finally, I spotted my friend Petunia Prettypaws pedaling by on her bike. I waved but she didn't see me. She just stared straight ahead with a sleepy, glazed look in her eyes. What was going on?

A chill ran down my fur, and this time it wasn't from the cold! A minute later I heard the sound of flapping wings . . .

FLAP! FLAP! FLAP!

It felt like someone was tapping me on the shoulder. A ghost? I shivered. Then I spotted a

snow-white feather

on the ground. I picked it up.

I wondered where the feather came from, but there was no time to figure it out. I was late!

At last, I arrived at *The Rodent's Gazette*. **FROZEN FUR BALLS**! I almost forgot to introduce myself! In case you don't already know, my name is Stilton, *Geronimo Stilton*. I am the publisher of *The Rodent's Gazette*, the most famouse newspaper on Mouse Island!

SNORE . . . ZZZZZZ!

Where was I? Ah yes, I was standing at the door to my office when I heard the most peculiar sound. **ZZZZZZZZ!** It sounded like a whole bunch of mice snoring. How strange.

I entered the office and gasped. Almost everyone was sleeping! What a **SNoreFest**!

I hated to break up the **slumber party**, but how else could I find out what was going on? So I cleared my throat and squeaked really loudly, "Good morning, everyone!"

My coworkers woke up with a start, rubbing their eyes and complaining,

"What a terrible sleep I had last night!"

"Me, too!"

"I dreamed of strange fairies dressed in **black**!"

"Me, too—they were playing *silver violins*!"

Everyone gathered around trying to figure out why they all seemed to be having the same **CRAZY NIGHTMARE**.

I listened, but I didn't say a word. I was thinking. Could these dreams have something to do with **WITHER** and the **DARK FAIRIES**?

No, that wasn't possible! The dark fairies lived in the *Kingdom of Fantasy*, not in the real world!

Suddenly, a nagging thought hit me. A while ago I had misplaced the Winged Ring that Blossom the Queen of Fairies gave to me. It's the ring that can transport me to the *Kingdom of Fantasy*. Luckily, I found it and put it in my **NIGHTSTAND** drawer for safekeeping. But was it still there?

Ummmm . . .

No one on Mouse Island knew about the ring, but I was suddenly worried.

I scampered home to check on the enchanted ring.

Outside, the weather had gotten worse. The air was *freezing*. The FOG was thick. And the wind was so strong it was messing up my previously good fur day!

It was then that I heard that strange sound.

FLAP! FLAP! FLAP!

I turned around, but again I didn't see anything.

On the ground I spotted another feather as white as snow.

WHO? WHO? WHO?

Now I was really worried. Someone was following me!

I scampered inside and **LOCKED** the door behind me, shivering with fear.

Just when I thought things couldn't get any scarier I heard a sound . . . Tap! Tap! Tap!

Someone was tapping on my window!

Terrified, I looked out . . .

"Aaaah!" I screamed.

Outside the window there was a massive snowy white OWL staring at me with enormouse

golden eyes!

Around her neck she wore a sparkly golden pendant.

The owl flapped her wings . . .

FLAP! FLAP! FLAP!

Her eyes never blinked.

So that's who had been following me in the fog! But why?

I opened the window to stop the staring contest and right then a voice next to the owl called out, "Sir Knight, I mean Prince, I mean . . . well, do you have it?"

Huh? Who was out there and what were they looking for?

The voice croaked impatiently, "Okay, come on, what are you waiting for? Aren't you going to check?"

Only then did I recognize the voice. It belonged to SCRIBBLEHOPPER, my frog friend and my first official guide to the Kingdom of Fantasy!

I stuck my snout out into the clouds to see if I could spot him and shrieked.

A crab's claw reached out and PINCHED my nose!

OUCHHHH!

Ouuuch!

Come on, Sir Knight!

It was **Chatterclaws**, another old friend from the Kingdom of Fantasy! Chatterclaws was a descendant of the renowned Crustacean Dynasty and worked for the queen as a *royal marine messenger*.

"How's it going, Prince?" he asked, but before I could open my mouth he chattered on. "Nah, tell me later, we're in a rush here. WHatSHeRface, I mean Queen Blossom, is waiting. So go get the WHATCHAMACALLIT, I mean the Winged Ring, and let's go!"

"Well, um, sure, er, but what's going on?" I stammered.

Right then a tall knight with a long **blue cape** climbed through my window. It was **BLUE RIDER**, another friend from (surprise, surprise!) the Kingdom of Fantasy!

"Hello, mouse, I have **ARRIVED!**

Everything's under control!" he declared.

Now, I must confess, when I first met **Blue Rider** I thought he was a total braggart. His favorite saying is, "**I am the best of the best!**"

I have arrived!

But since then I have learned that he has a *HUGE* heart. He spends his days defending the HELPLESS and the **HOPELESS**. What's more selfless than that?

What's going on?

Blue Rider

is the son of Azul, the Ancient One with the Sapphire eyes. He met Geronimo on his sixth adventure to the Kingdom of Fantasy. He is known as the hero of the hopeless. He likes to say he is the best of the best (not to mention daring, courageous, and charming)!

A Crow's Feather!

Blue **waved** his sword in the air and reminded me about the Winged Ring. "Where is it?" he asked.

I turned on my bedroom light and led Blue over to my nightstand table. Then I opened the drawer and . . . **gasped**! The ring was missing!

Blue Rider stared at the empty drawer and observed, "I don't see a ring in this nightstand."

"But . . . but . . . but . . . that's where I put it!" I cried.

Scribblehopper popped out from behind Blue Rider and croaked, "Wait, you put a *precious* object in the drawer of a nightstand? Seriously?"

Then he picked up a *feather* as **black** as ink that was next to the nightstand. "Hey, look at this! It's a **crow's** feather!" he declared.

This is a crow's feather!

Next, he pointed to **tracks** near the nightstand. "That looks like the clawprint of a **crow**!" he went on.

Finally, he pointed to a peck mark on the nightstand. "And that looks like a **crow's** peck mark!" he finished.

This is a crow's print!

So it was a crow who **stole** the ring!

But how?

Blue Rider gasped. "This can only be the work of the **evil** and legendary . . .

And this is a crow's peck mark!

CROWBAR THE CRUEL!

"Oh no!" Chatterclaws wailed. "Scribblehopper is right, Prince! Why would you put the enchanted ring in a whatchamacallit, I mean, nightstand drawer? What were you thinking? Who would leave a precious thingamabob, er, treasure, in a drawer? Any evil, rotten, no-good criminal could steal it! Or maybe . . ."

Blue Rider interrupted Chatterclaws with a wave of his sword. Thank goodness! That crab could go on for hours if you let him!

"You need to come with us to the *Kingdom of Fantasy*!" Blue declared. "This is serious!"

I didn't really understand how losing the enchanted ring could cause major problems, so my friends explained it to me.

Apparently, the Winged Ring was pure crystalized energy and gave enormouse power to whoever owned it. Thanks to me, once Wither got her hands on the ring, her powers

CROWBAR THE CRUEL

In the Kingdom of Witches, in an enormouse dried-out baobab tree, live 333 crows that are so dark you can't even see them at night! They have shiny copper beaks that are as sharp as razors because they sharpen them every morning at dawn. These crows are cruel and deceitful. Beware if you meet one. They cannot be trusted!

The prince of these dark crows is called Crowbar the Cruel. They say that he is capable of stealing anything. For this reason the dark fairy Wither ordered him to steal the Winged Ring from Geronimo.

In addition to stealing, Crowbar is said to have another talent. He is capable of changing shape. He can transform from a crow to a knight, depending on the situation.

Rumor has it, Crowbar is engaged to marry Wither. What a rotten pair that would be!

multiplied by **1,000 percent**! The energy from the ring also opened up a PASSAGE between the real world and the Kingdom of Fantasy. Gulp! Was Wither about to invade Mouse Island with her dark fairy army?

Scribblehopper croaked, "Didn't you notice this morning that things have already started to change in your world? Didn't you wonder why there was all this fog in the springtime? Didn't you see all of the black crows flapping all over the place? Didn't you smell that DISGUSTING sulfur smell? You know, it smells like rotten eggs? You can't miss it. Hmmm, have you thought about seeing a doctor? Maybe you need to get your Sniffer checked out."

LET'S GET HOPPING!

 h what a nightmare! Why hadn't I put that ring in a safe?

"Well, let's get hopping! If we leave now, we'll reach the CRYSTAL CASTLE by dawn!" Scribblehopper said.

"Prepare to defend yourself," Blue Rider added. "The Fairy Court will judge you for your foolish actions."

At this, Chatterclaws BURST into tears. He blew his nose on my tie.

"Oh, Prince, this is the saddest day in my entire whatchamacallit, life!" the crab wailed. "The Fairy Court will **skewer** you! But don't worry, I promise to come visit you in the you-know-what, **prison**, every single day. Well, okay, maybe not every day. I like to spend the weekends with my lovely wife, **CLassyclaws**. And not on Tuesdays or Wednesdays, 'cause that's when I like to go digging for treasure. And Mondays and Thursdays I rearrange the furniture in the Chatterhouse and . . ."

Scribblehopper covered the crab's mouth. "Quiet, you'll scare him. Don't tell him that almost everyone in the Kingdom of Fantasy is mad at him! Don't tell him they will throw **rotten tomatoes** at him! Don't tell him that they changed his name from *Prince Geronimo of Stilton* to the FOOLISH ONE, *the Mouse Who Lost the Winged Ring*!"

Blue Rider slung his arm around my shoulders. "It's okay, FOOLISH ONE," he said. "I am your friend and I will try to **defend** you in court even though it won't be easy."

"He can't go to the *Kingdom of Fantasy* in that suit and tie. He needs a **Disguise**," Scribblehopper observed. He raced out of the room and returned lugging a huge **chest** behind him. Huh? Where did that come from?

I didn't have time to ask. The chest had something etched in Fantasian* on it.

*You will find the Fantasian alphabet on page 571 at the end of the book.

There are a lot of disguises in here!

"I think he should dress like a whatsitcalled, lobster!" Chatterclaws suggested.

Lobster

"No, he should dress like a frog!" Scribblehopper insisted.

Chatterclaws **pinched** his nose. "No way, frogface! It would be much better if he dresses like a slimy pile of whatchamacallit, algae!" the crab yelled.

Frog

"**RIDICULOUS!**" Scribblehopper responded, hopping up and down in anger. "He'd be much more believable if he dressed up like a *lily pad*!"

Pile of algae

Before long, the two them began to fight, proposing all kinds of disguises, one more absurd than the next.

"He should dress like a blowfish!"

"No, a dragonfly!"

Lily pad

Finally, Blue Rider cut them short. "That's enough! FOOLISH ONE doesn't need to attract attention. He should dress like a plain old **traveling mouse**."

Foolish One

Blue Rider dug around in the chest and pulled out a green tunic, a hat with a **RED** feather, a hooded cape, and a leather bag.

As soon as I changed I heard the sound of wings.

FLAP! FLAP! FLAP!

Outside, the snowy owl was waiting. Then we climbed on her back and she took off, soaring HIGHER AND HIGHER INTO THE CLOUDS

FLAP
FLAP
FLAP
FLAP
FLAP
owl

As we flew, a **dark shadow** suddenly descended upon us. It was an enormouse crow with a **copper beak**, with feathers as black as ink and sparkling eyes.

He stuck out his **sharp talons** to grab me, but Blue Rider slashed the evil bird's foot with his sword.

"**Cawww!** How dare you attack Crowbar the Cruel!" he yelled angrily. "Crowbar will make you pay for this! **Cawww!**"

Then he turned and flew away into the **gloomy** night.

How many feathers is the owl losing?

Answer on page 572

In the sky there was a dark cyclone that spun and spun and spun around and around and around

Rancid cheese rinds! That twister stunk like rotten eggs! Oh, why hadn't I brought my nose plugs? Have you tried them? I use them sometimes when I'm taking out stinky trash.

Anyway, where was I? Oh yes, I was headed for the *Kingdom of Fantasy*. As we flew,

thunder CRASHED, LIGHTNING FLASHED.

Finally, at dawn we spotted the CRYSTAL CASTLE.

THE KINGDOM OF FANTASY

Where Foolish One faced a thousand adventures and a thousand dangers to find the precious Winged Ring . . .

KINGDOM OF FANTASY

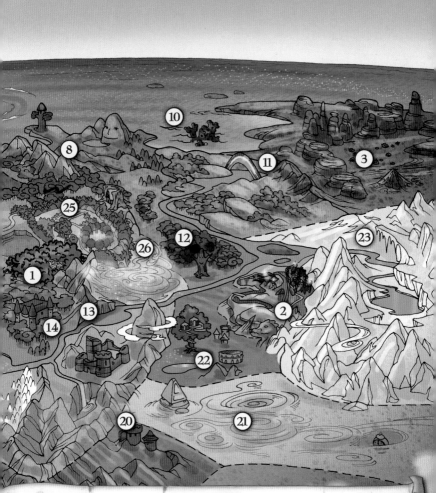

1. Kingdom of the Invisible Spiders
2. Empire of the Ruby Dragons
3. Desert of Eyes and Ears
4. Land of a Thousand Shadows
5. Land of Nightmares
6. Kingdom of the Fire Dragons
7. Kingdom of the Pixies
8. Kingdom of the Gnomes
9. Kingdom of the Fairies
10. Kingdom of the Sea
11. Rainbow Valley
12. Talking Forest
13. Kingdom of the Northern Giants
14. Kingdom of the Elves
15. Kingdom of the Diggerts
16. Land of Trolls
17. Kingdom of the Witches
18. Land of Sweets
19. Land of the Ogres
20. Kingdom of the Southern Giants
21. Land of Time
22. Kingdom of the Silver Dragons
23. Realm of the Towering Peaks
24. Land of Toys
25. Green County
26. Bright Empire

1. Rose of a Thousand Petals
2. Glittering Lake
3. Woods of Goodness
4. Pretty-Shade Plain
5. Pink Forest
6. Turquoise House
7. Flowery Mountain
8. Tooth Fairy's Manor
9. Fountain of Youth
10. Silver Abyss
11. Fairy Godmother's Tower
12. Mountain of Sweet Dreams
13. Mountain of Secrets
14. Crystal Castle
15. Sweetwater Lake
16. Bright Hopes Way
17. Green Gate
18. Fairy Quarter
19. Happy Trails Station
20. Gazebo of Love
21. Petal Way
22. The Forest of Nymphs

KINGDOM OF THE FAIRIES

The Magical World of the Fairies

☆Who is Queen Blossom of the Flowers?☆

Blossom is the Queen of the Fairies. She lives in her Royal Palace known as the Crystal Castle. Blossom is the heart of the Kingdom of Fantasy. Her wish is to bring peace and happiness to the entire kingdom.

☆The Dynasty of the Winged Ones☆

Blossom belongs to the Dynasty of the Winged Ones, the founders of the Kingdom of Fantasy. Her sister, Wither, has passed to the Dark Side . . . and has become her most dangerous enemy!

☆The Making of Sir Geronimo of Stilton☆

The Kingdom of Fantasy has been in danger many times. Every time, Blossom has called Geronimo Stilton to help her. Because of his loyalty Geronimo has been named Knight of the Silver Rose; Knight of the Treasured Gemstones; and Fearless, Prince of the Winged Ones, among other things. Blossom and Geronimo are now BFFs!

☆ *The Great Fairy Council* ☆

Queen Blossom is powerful, but still she must obey the Great Fairy Council, or Fairy Court, which is made up of the seven wisest fairies of the kingdom. Judge Strictwings leads the court. She is tough but fair.

THE LAWS OF THE KINGDOM OF FAIRIES

1. *Every fairy must respect the laws of the Kingdom of Fairies.*

2. *Every fairy must obey the Great Fairy Council.*

3. *Every fairy will only use magic powers for good.*

4. *The greater a fairy's magical powers, the greater the fairy's responsibility.*

5. *Every fairy must defend the Kingdom of Fairies, even if it is dangerous.*

6. *Every fairy must protect the secrets of the Kingdom of Fantasy from those who might misuse them.*

7. *Every fairy who breaks the laws will lose all fairy powers and will be exiled forever.*

WHAT A FURBRAIN!

As we approached the Crystal Castle, I began to make out the shimmering towers and blue flags. I couldn't wait to see Blossom. In fact, for a second, I thought I spotted her behind a window.

The owl landed in front of the castle. A huge crowd made up of the inhabitants of the Kingdom of Fantasy had gathered. What a nice welcoming committee, I thought . . . until it hit me!

Splat! That's right, someone in the crowd had thrown a ***rotten tomato*** at me!

"It's him!" the crowd cried.

"It's FOOLISH ONE, the mouse who lost the ring!"

"Now the Kingdom of Fantasy is in **danger**, because Wither stole it!"

"I heard he kept the ring in a nightstand drawer. What a **furbrain**!"

I was in shock. At one time, *everyone* in the Kingdom of Fantasy loved me. They even considered me a hero. Now they thought I was a traitor!

Rat-munching rattlesnakes! How could I have SUNK SO low?

Luckily, Blue Rider drew his sword. "Leave FOOLISH ONE alone, or you'll have to deal with me!" he warned.

Blue Rider led me to the back of the castle. He knocked on a door and a peephole opened. "Umm, are you friends or enemies?" a little voice asked.

Can you see where Queen Blossom is?

"Friends!" Blue Rider responded.

"Umm, do you have a pass?" the voice continued.

Blue slipped a rolled-up scroll in the peephole.

"Umm, so what's the password?" the voice added.

Let me in!

"Oh, give me a break! You know me, **Boils**! It's Blue Rider! Now let me in!" the knight demanded.

At that point the little door opened and a green face peeked out that I, too,

recognized. It was

**Boils
the chameleon!**

"Sorry, but you know you can never be too careful! These are dangerous times here in the kingdom," he said.

Boils

is a little chameleon who changes colors to blend with his surroundings. In the past, he worked as a spy for the trolls and for the Queen of the Witches. Then he met Geronimo and changed his ways. Fun fact: Boils will do anything for candy!

Here is the map of Crystal Castle, Blossom's palace, at the time of our arrival!

Snowy White

Lab for making fairy dust

Strongheart

Fairy kitchen

Stairway

Entryway

Wardrobe

Rightwings

Wrongwings

Courtwings

Strictwings

Fibwings

Truthwings

Rulewings

Room of spells

King Skywings

Greenhouse for cultivating roses

Collection of flower scents

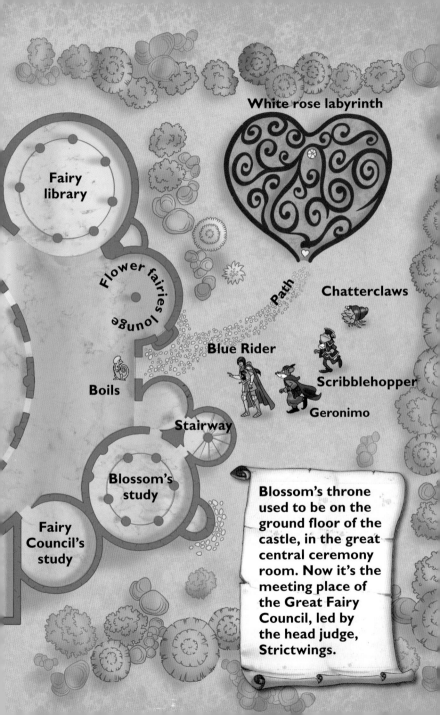

White rose labyrinth

Fairy library

Flower fairies lounge

Path

Chatterclaws

Blue Rider

Scribblehopper

Boils

Geronimo

Stairway

Blossom's study

Fairy Council's study

Blossom's throne used to be on the ground floor of the castle, in the great central ceremony room. Now it's the meeting place of the Great Fairy Council, led by the head judge, Strictwings.

BLOSSOM'S SECRET QUARTERS

I was nervous after the tomato-throwing bit, but I entered the castle and followed Blue Rider down a hallway to a painting of **Blossom**.

The knight looked around to check for spies, then he put his hand on the painting. It spun around,

This way!

A secret passage!

revealing a PASSAge that led to the SECRET QUARTERS of the Queen of the Fairies!

The **smell of roses** filled the air. And there before me was **Queen Blossom**! "Welcome back to the Kingdom of Fantasy, my friend," she said.

Whew! Well, that was a relief. At least Blossom wasn't going to start pelting me with **overripe tomatoes**. Still, I could tell by her expression that she wasn't going to throw me a party, either.

"My Queen, I am here to set things right," I squeaked.

She smiled sadly and said, "I know you didn't mean it. But you did not take proper care of the Winged Ring. It was no ordinary ring, and you left it in the drawer of your nightstand."

What could I say? The queen was right. I should have put the ring in a locked box in my basement (except I don't have a basement). Or I could have put it in my refrigerator in a hollowed-out

CRYSTAL CASTLE

1. Ceremony Room
2. Blossom's Room
3. Fairy Bathroom
4. Open Aviary
5. Roses Greenroom
6. Library
7. Embroidery Room
8. Secret Study
9. Secret Meeting Room
10. Maid Quarters
11. Music Room
12. Kitchens
13. Guest Room
14. Hanging Garden
15. Dining Room
16. Safe
17. Private Bathroom
18. Personal Wardrobe

chunk of cheese (although I might have eaten it by accident). Well, either way, I **MESSED** up!

"I'm sorry," I squeaked.

Blossom shook her head. "It's okay." She sighed. "I never imagined Wither would have the courage to reach you all the way in Mouse Island!"

Then she added, "Even worse, I just found

If only I had been more careful . . .

It's okay . . .

out that Wither has called together the Great Witch Council to elect a new Queen of the Witches!"

Huh? That didn't make **SENSE**. "But isn't

Cackle

their queen? And Wither is her friend, right?" I asked.

"Not exactly. You see, friendship and loyalty don't exist between witches," Blossom explained. "Instead of being thankful to Cackle for raising and protecting her, **WITHER** is now trying to steal her throne! The Winged Ring has multiplied her magic powers by 1,000 percent. But let me explain the story of the legendary ring so you will understand why it's so important . . ."

The Story of the Winged Ring

This is the true story. No, really, don't believe anything else that anyone tells you!

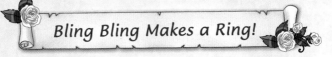

Bling Bling Makes a Ring!

The ring was designed for the first of the Winged Ones, King Regal. The king asked Gnome Bling Bling, the Master Jeweler, to make the ring since he was the expert in making magic jewelry. Bling mixed silver extract from all the lands of the Kingdom of Fantasy so that everyone could control it. Then he fused it with the fire from all the volcanoes so its power could reach the heart of whoever wore it. Then he molded it in the waters of all the lands for purity and dried it with the air of all the winds so that its power would have no limits. Finally, Bling decorated it with scented rose so that it smelled like a freshly picked flower.

Ring Power!

The Winged Ring multiplies the power
of whoever wears it by 1,000 percent!
It should only be worn by Winged Ones
or those whose hearts are pure.

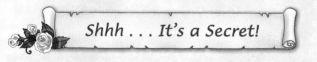

Shhh . . . It's a Secret!

The ring has a secret. It is made up of perfectly
equal measurements that match the golden
ratio of everything that exists in nature.

A Nightstand?

Right then I heard a voice echo through the castle. "The Great Fairy Council is now called to order! **Blossom** and FOOLISH ONE, present yourselves before the

Great Fairy Court!"

"This is it," Blossom said, leading me down a long, twisting crystal corridor. First we turned left, then right, then right again, then left. I'm telling you, this place was a total maze! For a minute I thought we might be lost forever! Oh, what a **NIGHTMARE**!

Finally, we ended up in the enormouse ceremony room. There were eight fairies seated on chairs in front of us. Above them hung a plaque that said in Fantasian*, `Fairy Law is the same for all.` JUDGE STRICTWINGS swore us in. "Do you swear to tell the truth and nothing but the truth?"

When we agreed, she ordered us to sit.

Blossom sat down and fairy Rulewings began to question her.

I swear!

Do you swear to tell the truth?

Strictwings the fairy judge

*You will find the Fantasian alphabet on page 571.

The Ceremony Room

Poor Blossom . . .

It's all Foolish One's fault!

"**Is it true** that you, Your Majesty, gave the Winged Ring to this rodent?"

Blossom whispered, "Yes, it's true."

Rulewings continued, "**Is it true** that you told this rodent that he should take care of it?"

Blossom sighed. "Yes, it's true."

Rulewings insisted, "**Is it true** that he brought the ring to the real world and put it in the drawer of his nightstand and Wither stole it?"

Blossom tried to defend me, "Yes, **it's true**, but it was all my fault. I should have WARNED him . . ."

Then Rulewings quoted FAIRY LAW #6, which states,

*You can find the Fantasian alphabet on page 571.

Υ৳ᛎ□◑৳ ϘᏇৡᏇ ᛎⵜ ⵜↆ↑↳

This writing is on the Fairy Court's desk. Try to translate it.*

"EVERY FAIRY MUST PROTECT THE SECRETS OF THE KINGDOM OF FANTASY FROM THOSE WHO MIGHT MISUSE THEM."

Because Blossom had broken law #6, the judge said she could be **exiled** forever!

Everyone watching the trial gasped in horror. At the same time they seemed to be shooting **daggers** in my direction. I felt a mouse-sized headache coming on. It was my fault the queen was in trouble!

Before I could think, the judge had turned her attention to me. She asked me my name, my address, my phone number, my height, my weight, and if I liked PIZZA or STEAK. I answered all of her questions, even if they seemed a little strange. I mean, what mouse doesn't prefer pizza?

Finally, the judge got around to the reason I had been called before the council.

"Is it true that you received the Winged Ring from Queen Blossom, but instead of keeping it in a safe place, you put it in the DRAWER of a nightstand?" she asked. "I mean, what were you thinking? Who puts something so precious in an unlocked drawer? I could see if you put a flashlight or a book in your drawer, but

TRIALWINGS   WRONGWINGS   TRUTHWINGS   FIBWINGS

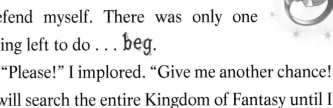

an **enchanted ring**? Really?"

Rats! This was all my fault. I couldn't defend myself. There was only one thing left to do . . . **beg**.

"Please!" I implored. "Give me another chance! I will search the entire Kingdom of Fantasy until I find the Winged Ring! I will **CLIMB** every mountain. I will *swim* every ocean. Well, maybe I'll take a boat. I'm not the best swimmer. Still, I'll find it!"

"We will return with our **decision**," said Strictwings, leading the fairies out of the room.

| COURTWINGS | RIGHTWINGS | RULEWINGS | STRICTWINGS |

THE SECRET ALLIANCE

As we waited for the fairies to return, I approached Blossom. "Your Majesty, I promise I can fix this **mess**!" I squeaked.

Blossom lowered her voice, "Only one thing can save us. You need to ask the help of the three members of the Secret Alliance:

The Clever Chameleon

and the

Lady of Dreams."

"Okay, great! Where can I find them?" I asked.

"First you must reach the BRIGHT EMPIRE where all the wizards and sorcerers of the Kingdom of Fantasy live. There you will find Mel the Magnificent, the Clever Chameleon, and the Lady of Dreams."

Mel the Magnificent

The Clever Chameleon

The Lady of Dreams

I jumped to my paws, ready to take off, but the queen grabbed my paw. She insisted I listen to her story explaining the secret alliance she had formed with the three wizards.

It went something like this . . .

The Story of the Secret Alliance

A thousand years ago, Cackle chose Mel the Magnificent for her husband . . .

What a catch!

We could take over the Kingdom of Fantasy!

She wanted to unite the power of the witches and the power of the wizards.

But Mel wasn't interested . . .

I'm not interested in power . . . or you!

How dare you!

Cackle grew furious and decided to seek revenge . . .

She led an attack on the Bright Empire . . .

You will pay for refusing me!

Mel gathered all the wizards of the Bright Empire. He asked for help from the two most powerful . . . the Clever Chameleon and the Lady of Dreams.

We need to stop the witches!
They are so evil . . .

But they weren't able to stop the evil witches . . .

They are too strong!
We can't do it!

Cackle's troops surrounded the Bright Empire . . .

Attack them, my warriors! We will win!

I, Blossom, the Queen of Fairies, order you to leave!

But then I, Blossom, came to help . . .

And that is how our secret alliance began . . .

How can we repay you, dear Queen?

Sparkle Flower

After Blossom finished telling her story, she showed me a *pendant* that she wore around her neck. It was made of four of the purest **BLUE CRYSTALS**, which sparkled like stars.

"When you meet my friends, show them this pendant so they recognize you. It is called Sparkle Flower, the pendant of the secret alliance! We each have one," she explained.

It seemed kind of SiLLy to name a pendant, but I didn't want to insult the queen, so I just nodded.

"Take care not to lose the pendant, Foolish One," Blossom continued. "It represents the **PoweR of fRieNDShip**. It will bring you courage in your darkest moments."

Then the queen gave me a map and explained

how to reach the Bright Empire. Believe me, it didn't sound easy. First I had to take the Road of Illuminated Hope, away from the City of Fairies. Then I had to follow it in the same direction that the sun rises (east!), and then I would walk along toward Green County. There I would reach the GREEN GATE and enter the Green Forest and continue on the Green Path until I found the Circle of the Twelve Green Guardians. After I passed some kind of test the guardians gave me, I could enter the

BRIGHT EMPIRE!

Whew! I was exhausted just thinking about this journey! Still, I put the pendant around my neck and promised to do my best.

Sparkle Flower

This flower-shaped pendant is made up of four of the purest sky-colored quartz crystals. Nothing can darken its splendor, because it reflects the rays of the sun like a mirror. Its light will light up the heart and mind of whoever wears it!

THE SECRET ALLIANCE

Blossom, the Lady of Dreams, Mel the Magnificent, and the Clever Chameleon represent the four virtues that give strength to the secret alliance.

Purity

Strength

Fantasy

Wisdom

Blossom
of the Flowers

PURITY

Blossom is also known as the Flower Queen, the Lady of Peace and Happiness, She Who Brings Harmony. She is the Queen of the Fairies and of all of the Kingdom of Fantasy.

Her skin shines of crystalline light. Rosebuds and diamonds are braided in her hair. She seems very young, and yet her reign has lasted an infinite time!

Blossom of the Flowers, within the secret alliance, embodies the virtue of PURITY. Only a pure heart can understand what is just.

Mel the Magnificent

STRENGTH

Mel is called the Magnificent because he is the most powerful wizard in all of the Kingdom of Fantasy. Throughout his long life he has dedicated himself to the study of the Magic Arts, traveling far and wide through the Kingdom (that is how he learned all of the known languages!).

In addition to the golden crown, he always carries his trusted Wandress, the most powerful magic wand that exists (he is the only one who can control it!) and the Magicarium, his Book of Magic Spells.

Mel embodies the virtue of STRENGTH. Only a strong mind can work on Magical Studies without desiring power.

The Lady of Dreams

The Lady of Dreams has skin as white as snow, a mouth as red as a cherry, eyes as blue as cornflowers, and hair as golden as wheat . . . She reigns over the marvemouse Mountain of Sweet Dreams, which is always covered in soft, fluffy clouds. No one has ever visited the mountain, but anyone can dream about it. Go ahead! Can you picture it?

The Lady of Dreams is the member of the secret alliance who embodies the virtue of FANTASY. *Anyone with an imagination is lucky because they will always have hope. They can dream of answers that others cannot see and best of all they can dream in vivid color!*

THE CLEVER CHAMELEON

Born in the Thousand-Year Land, Clever, also known as Clev, is a member of the Lizard Population. His skin is leathery, his scales sparkle, and as a chameleon he can match his color to the surrounding environment and become invisible. He is a master of all martial arts, and invented the Study of the Split Tongue. Using the vibrations of certain words, he can strike his enemies as if he were using a powerful sword. He can also fight using a wooden cane that transforms into a thousand different weapons.

The Clever Chameleon embodies the virtue of WISDOM. His strength is his experience throughout his life. All the leaders of the Kingdom of Fantasy seek his advice.

At that moment, the fairies returned to the ceremony room. I was a wreck! My **FATE** and that of the Kingdom of Fantasy depended on their response!

"Foolish One, you will now be sentenced!" Judge Strictwings announced.

My whiskers were trembling from the stress.
My whiskers were trembling from the stress.
My whiskers were trembling from the stress.

She continued, "We have decided it is your fault that the Winged Ring was stolen. But we have also decided to give you **a second chance**. You will leave at once to find the ring, but if you don't bring it back within one moon — that is twenty-nine days — Queen Blossom will be **exiled**. And a new queen — or a new king — will be crowned."

At those words the **ENORMOUSE** door of the Ceremony Room opened and the

Great Attendant

of the **Weaselly Weasels** entered. He wore a red coat with gold trim and a funny wig on his head.

SHAKING a small **golden bell**, he yelled, "Inhabitants of the Kingdom of Fantasy! Hear ye! Hear ye!"

Hear yeee! Hear yeeeeeeeee!

WILLARD THE WEASELLY

The room fell silent as the **weasel** continued to shout at full volume, "I am here to present the smartestest, noblestest, handsomestest, and all around bestest . . .

PRINCE WILLARD THE WEASELLY,

also known as Lord of the Spotted Fur, Hero of a Thousand Battles (or much less), Defender of the Furrybellies, and most of all . . . Taker of the Throne of the Kingdom of Fantasy!"

He stopped to catch his breath, then went on, "And with him, his sister will also make her entrance, the charmingestest . . .

PRINCESS WILLAMENA!"

Prince Willard entered the room with his nose held high. He had white fur, and his tail had a **black spot** on the end. He wore a velvet cape and carried what looked like a *royal scepter*. Willard's sister, Princess Willamena, was dressed in a fancy pink ball gown.

Make way!

Stand back!

Prince Willard the Weaselly

powdered wig

golden monocle

evil smile

thumb ring

curls set with scented gel

velvet cloak with pearls from the Mermaid Sea

pinky ring

scepter with a pink pearl as large as an egg

walking cane

tail with a black tip

lace handkerchief with his initials

His TITLES: Prince Willard the Weaselly of the Seven Tail Dynasty, Sire of the Thickcoats, Great Chomper of Perfect Pizzas, etc.

His PERSONALITY: He is convinced that he is the most intelligent, the most cunning, the most handsome in all the Kingdom of Fantasy! Don't tell him he's wrong!

His WEAKNESS: He loves pizza but tends to overeat and end up with a stomachache!

His SECRET: He is madly in love with Martina the marten weasel, known as Priss, Princess of the Rococo Dynasty.

Princess Willamena

powdered wig

fake mole

emerald necklace

velvet cloak with rubies

very precious rings

solid-gold fan

diamond tiara
evil smile

opera glasses

lace purse

tail with black tip

brocade dress

HER TITLES: Princess Willamena the Weaselly of the Seven Tail Dynasty

HER PERSONALITY: She is spoiled rotten and constantly scolds her pawmaids and her betrothed, Count Ferret.

HER WEAKNESS: She is so vain she spends half her day looking in the mirror.

HER SECRET: She has stinky breath — that's why she is always chewing on mints.

THE PRINCE'S LUGGAGE

1. Portable desk

2. Ceremony suit (ready for his crowning!)

3. Seven pairs of patent leather shoes, one for each day of the week

4. Seven wigs

5. Seven pairs of underwear and seven lace shirts

6. Toiletries

7. Silver dishes

8. Seven gala suits

9. Seven pairs of pajamas

10. Precious, solid-gold chamber pot

AND THE PRINCESS'S

1. Ceremony gown (ready for her crowning!)

2. Seven lace dresses, one for each day of the week

3. Seven pairs of patent leather shoes

4. Seven pairs of satin pajamas

5. Crystal glasses

6. Cup of vanilla-flavored hot chocolate

7. Personal pantry

8. Wigs

9. Toiletries

10. Seven gala gowns

11. Spy gear

I'VE GOT EVERYTHING!

illard turned to the crowd. Then he said in a high-pitched voice, "Citizens of the Kingdom of Fantasy, I am here to announce to you that I am ready to become the next

KING OF THE KINGDOM OF FANTASY!"

Everyone looked horrified. I wasn't surprised. Who would want a squeaky-voiced weasel as a ruler? Willard just yammered on and on. "I've got everything I need — the CROWN, the cape, the scepter, the charm, the wit, the invitations to the ceremony, and the pizza for the celebration!"

The crowd began to grumble, but Strictwings silenced them.

The judge thanked Willard for his offer but explained about her decision to give me another

Answer on page 572

How many gnomes are in the room?

chance. "Foolish One will have one moon's time to find the Winged Ring. If he fails, we will choose a new queen or king for the Kingdom," she told the weasel.

Willard looked as if he might explode. His eyes bugged out. His nostrils flared. Even his curls tightened in anger. He pointed at Blossom, "Excuse me, miss, but you should not be trusted. I mean, your twin sister is WITHER. I know your game!"

Then he pointed at me. "And you, rodent, are a disaster! They don't call you Foolish One for nothing!" he screeched, yanking my whiskers.

Youch!

You are a disaster!

Willamena joined in, "Yeah, we can't trust you!"

She stuck out her high-heeled shoe and **stomped** on my tail.

Double youch!

We can't trust you!

Then Willard bonked me on the head with his scepter as Willamena thwacked her fan on my ears.

Triple youch!

Take this . . .

And this!

"Please," I begged Strictwings. "Don't listen to them. I promise I'll return. Rodent's honor."

The fairy stared at me for a **LONG** time. In fact, she stared at me for so **LONG** I started to get self-conscious. Was it my fur? Did I have something in my **TEETH**?

At last, she banged her gavel and declared, "Foolish One, I believe you are truthful. You will leave now to find the ring, and you will return within **ONE MOON**!"

LUNAR CYCLES

1	2	3	4
NEW MOON	FIRST QUARTER	FULL MOON	LAST QUARTER

The moon takes approximately twenty-nine days to complete its cycle around the earth. During this time it looks different depending on what part of it is lit by the sun.

"Oh, brother," the prince of the weasels huffed. "Now I've heard everything. That mouse will never come back. **Liar, liar, pants on fire**!"

"You said it," his sister agreed. "Just look at him. Who could trust that **shifty** face?"

But Strictwings didn't listen. She adjourned the court.

As the fairies were leaving, **Blossom** hugged me. "Good-bye! Good luck! And please be careful,

Good-bye!

I'll be back!

my friend!" she said.

I smiled. Don't get me wrong, I was scared out of my fur, but I didn't want to look like a scaredy-mouse. So I waved good-bye and took off for the BRIGHT EMPIRE.

Would I make it?

Who knows.

I was sure of only one thing.

I would do **everything** I could to make it back alive!

FOOLISH ONE'S JOURNEY

Where it is told of how he followed the Road of Illuminated Hope and reached Green County . . .

It's All Foolish One's Fault!

left the Kingdom of Fairies feeling scared but hopeful. Sure, the journey would be **DANGEROUS** but at least I had a map. What? Did you forget? Blossom had given me a MAP detailing the path I would need to reach the **BRIGHT EMPIRE**.

I pulled the **hood** of my cape over my head so no one would recognize me. Then I checked my bag. It contained everything I would need for the trip: bread, cheese, a cup, utensils, a flint rock for lighting **FIRES**, seven fairy flowers, and a king-sized bed. Well, okay, I didn't bring the bed, but that would have been **COZY**.

Ah yes, I was headed off on the long, winding

Here is the map that Blossom gave me!

This way for the Kingdom of the Gnomes

This way to the Kingdom of the Pixies

Green County

Kingdom of the Elves

The Road of Illuminated Hope

This way for the Kingdom of Trolls

Cut-off street

Fear Gorge

Enchanted City

Road of Illuminated Hope

As I trudged along, I did my best to **blend** in with the other inhabitants of the *Kingdom of Fantasy* heading along the same road.

They were all gossiping about Wither, Blossom, Prince Willard the Weaselly Weasel, and you-know-who. (Shh! I mean, **me** of course!)

"I wonder if we will get a new queen or king?"

"Too bad. Blossom was the best!"

What trouble he made!

Poor Blossom!

It's all Foolish One's fault!

What a furbrain!

It's all his fault!

"Yeah, she was GENEROUS and KIND and beautiful . . ."

"It's all Foolish One's fault!"

"What a **furbrain**!"

I sighed. They were right. It was all my fault. I felt lower than the lowest sewer rat.

I walked on and on for seven days and seven nights. Cheese sticks, I was tired! At night I had **TERRIBLE NIGHTMARES** where I saw the dark fairies and heard their sad music.

Grunt!

Alas!

Humph!

That fool caused a lot of trouble!

Oh, that tune made my whiskers tremble!

Can you see all thirty-three dark fairies in Geronimo's dream?

Answer on page 572

Caww! Cawww! Cawwww!

Before long, I had finished all the food Blossom had given me. I walked along the road with my stomach growling up a storm. If only I had taken a few cheesy PROtein bars for the road!

It was then that I saw an old, familiar bird fly by. It was the slyest raven in the Kingdom of Fantasy . . .

CLEVERWING!

Even though I was dressed in my disguise, he recognized me immediately. "**CAW!** Well, look at that! If it isn't my old pal the **MOUSE PRINCE**!" he squawked. "But wait, I heard you are no longer called knight or Sir Geronimo.

What do they call you . . . Simpletonsnout? Or was it Forgetfulface?"

One thing you should know about Cleverwing: He is a total **wise guy**! Still, I needed his help, so I didn't protest. You see, Cleverwing carried with him at all times a **golden chest**. Inside, he sold all types of merchandise.

"I could use . . ." I began.

He interrupted me. "Put on the breaks, stop, halt. I know what you need . . . a **NEW DISGUISE**!"

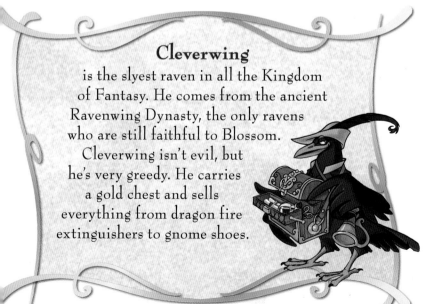

Cleverwing

is the slyest raven in all the Kingdom of Fantasy. He comes from the ancient Ravenwing Dynasty, the only ravens who are still faithful to Blossom. Cleverwing isn't evil, but he's very greedy. He carries a gold chest and sells everything from dragon fire extinguishers to gnome shoes.

*You will find the Fantasian alphabet on page 571.

"Even a freshly hatched raven just out of the egg would recognize you!" he continued. "What you need is an authentic secondhand **APPLE TREE** costume. It comes complete with moss, worms, snails, red ants, and a bird's nest. It costs five gold fairy coins. **It's a deal! Take it or leave it!**"

To convince me, he pulled out a wanted **poster** written in Fantasian with my face on it.*

"Okay, but actually I need provisions as well," I explained.

The bird snickered. "All right, then I will propose a deal. I will sell you the disguise for five gold coins and if you give me two more coins, I will give you my provisions! And, as a **FREE GIFT** with purchase, a book of raven recipes . . .

"Take it or leave it, Cawww!"

I accepted and gave Cleverwing seven of the **gold coins** that Blossom had given me.

He helped me put on the tree disguise. "Careful not to bend over. If you do, you'll lose the **eggs** in the nest," he warned.

He gave me the bundle with his provisions, adding, "Here's a little bit of free advice: If I were you, I'd watch my bag. As soon as you enter Green County you'll meet a bunch of little thieving **SPRITES**!

"Squirmy worms, you can barely see them, you furbrain! They are sprites wearing **Green Leaves**! If they see you pass by they won't think twice about snagging your bag!" He snorted before taking off. "Caww! It's a pleasure tricking . . . I

mean doing **business** with you, Foolish One!"

After he left I opened the bundle and . . . my apples **fell** in disappointment!

Yum! Here are the provisions!

Huh?

ROACHES WITH FLY BITS
(SPAGHETTI WITH OLIVES AND CHEESE)

A CLASSIC FIRST COURSE

INGREDIENTS:

For four people: 1 box of spaghetti, ½ jar of tomato sauce, 1 can of sliced black olives, 1 cup shredded mozzarella cheese, ½ cup grated Parmesan, 1 tbs olive oil, pinch of salt

DIRECTIONS:

With the help of an adult, put four quarts of water in a pot. Add olive oil and salt. Bring water to a boil, stirring frequently. Cook spaghetti until desired tenderness, about 8–10 minutes.

When pasta is cooked, drain and return to pot. Add mozzarella and olives. Heat until cheese is softened.

In a separate pot, heat up sauce, then pour over finished pasta. Serve with grated Parmesan.

ROACH MEATBALLS WITH EARTHWORM SAUCE
(MEATBALLS WITH SAUCE)

A DELICIOUS SECOND COURSE

INGREDIENTS:
for four people: 1 pound ground beef, 2 eggs, 2 tbs grated Parmesan, 1/2 cup bread crumbs, 1/4 minced onion, 1/2 tsp salt, 1/8 tsp ground black pepper, 1/2 jar of tomato sauce

DIRECTIONS:

With the help of an adult, combine the eggs, water, bread crumbs, onion, salt, and pepper. Add the ground beef and mix. from this mixture mold into round balls about 1 inch in diameter and place on a broiler pan.

Bake at 350 degrees for 25–30 minutes. Heat sauce in separate pot, pour over finished meatballs, and enjoy!

CLEVERWING'S JOKEY JOKES

What do worms leave around their baths?
The scum of the earth!

What kind of math do birds like?
Owlgebra!

Where do you put barking dogs?
In a barking lot!

Why don't fish like basketball?
They're afraid of the net!

Why do cows go to New York?
To see the moosicals!

What did the duck say when she bought lipstick?
Put it on my bill!

What do you call a wet bear?
A drizzly bear!

Why don't cats play cards in the jungle?
There are too many cheetahs!

What is a snake's favorite subject?
Hiss-story!

What do you call a pig that does karate?
A pork chop!

Why did the witches lose the baseball game?
Their bats flew away!

Where do mice park their boats?
At the hickory dickory dock!

THROUGH THE GREEN NIGHTMARE!

nd that is how, dressed as an apple tree, I continued my **JOURNEY** toward

GREEN COUNTY.

It was a terrible trip, because the tree costume was really uncomfortable!

The bark SCRATCHED my tail!

The **WORMS** tried to crawl in my ears!

The birds **pecked** at my head!

The RED ANTS pinched my paws!

Finally, at dawn, I found a **sign** in Fantasian* along the trail.

*You will find the Fantasian alphabet on page 571.

Aaack!

The sign pointed to a **PATH** that headed into the woods . . .

Soon I entered a thick forest of trees. The trees were so tall they barely let any sunlight in. A carpet of **dried leaves** covered the path, crunching under my pawsteps. **Crunch! Crunch!** Oh, what a fright!

At dawn on the third day I reached a clearing. For some reason the place gave me **chills**!

I could swear someone was watching me, but I couldn't see anyone!

Answer on page 573

I felt someone yank on my tail, pull my whiskers, and pinch my ears . . . but there was no one in sight!

Then I heard the RUSTLING

of branches and . . . someone stole my bag!

I had arrived at the CLEARING of the

LITTLE THIEVING SPRITES!

Even though my bag was gone I tried to give myself a pep talk. At least I still had Sparkle Flower, the magical pendant Blossom had given to me.

I walked . . . and walked . . . and walked . . .

until finally I reached an ENORMOUSE

The Little Thieving Sprites

live on the edges of Green County. They are so obnoxious that the other pixies kicked them out of the kingdom. Their king, Spriteness, is the cousin of Spratly of Sprets, the King of the Green Pixies.

The Thieving Sprites sew their clothes from green leaves, which makes them invisible in the forest. This helps them steal from anyone passing by!

KING OF THE LITTLE
THIEVING SPRITES

QUEEN OF THE LITTLE
THIEVING SPRITES

The Clearing of the Little Thieving Sprites

Can you find the Little Thieving Sprites hiding in the forest?

Where did my bag go?

Answer on page 573

tree whose branches were BRAIDED together to form a really tall gate. It was the

GREEN GATE OF GREEN COUNTY!

THE GREEN COUNTY

Where it is told of how Foolish One passed through the Green Gate, entered Green County, and met the Greenies . . .

The Green Gate

THE BAD
NEWS WAS . . .

The good news was: I made it to the gate. **The bad news was**: The gate was closed!

How would I enter? I felt a little silly, but I decided to ask the gate. "May I come in?" I asked politely.

Strangely, I had the feeling that the Green Gate was **WATCHING** me. And right at that moment it rumbled,

"WHO ARE YOUUUUU? AND WHAT DO YOU WAAAAANNNTTT?"

Gulp!

"I am the **PRINCE**, umm, I mean, I *was* the

prince, but well, now they call me FOOLISH ONE," I babbled. "I'm here on a very important mission for Queen Blossom. Will you open up and let me pass?"

"Well, Fooooolish One," the gate answered. "If you want to enter, you must solve the riddle of The Green Puzzler.

WHAT HAS ROOTS THAT NO ONE SEES, PASSES EVERY TREE, AND GOES UPWARD BUT NEVER GROWS?"

CHEESE AND CRACKERS!

I had no idea!

So I squeaked, "Well, to be honest, I don't understand a cheese rind of your puzzle so I'm just guessing here. Could it be a balloon? A watermelon? A STORM CLOUD?"

We have the answer
To the riddle,
Beginning, end, and
In the middle!

Chirp! Chirp!

Chirp! Chirp!

Chirp! Chirp!

Help Geronimo
solve the Green
Puzzler!

Answer on page 573

The gate stayed closed.

I thought about **breaking** down in sobs. Maybe the gate would feel sorry for me. But a minute later a group of friendly nightingales landed on my shoulders.

"We know the answer to the riddle," they said, whispering it in my ear.

I repeated it out loud and the Green Gate swung open.

WELCOME TO GREEN COUNTY!

GREEN COUNTY

Help Geronimo reach the Circle of the Twelve Green Guardians.

Geronimo

1. Forest of the Green Whippers
2. Forest of the Green Caners
3. Forest of the Green Biters
4. Forest of the Green Stingers
5. Forest of the Green Rushers
6. Forest of the Green Trippers
7. Forest of the Green Trappers
8. Twelve Green Guardians

Answer on page 573

THE SEVEN GREEN FORESTS

I found myself before the first forest, the forest of the **GREEN WHIPPERS**. Here grew trees that were like weeping willows, with really **long** branches that went down to the ground. Right then they began to **shake**. Next thing I knew a long branch reached out and **whacked** me in the tail! Now I understood why the forest was called the forest of the **GREEN WHIPPERS**!

Whack! Whack! Whack!

I ran quickly to the next grove of trees, the forest of the **GREEN CANERS**.

Too bad the second forest was just as bad as the first. The trees had **long** branches that were like THiN canes. They smacked me on the head!

SMACK! SMACK! SMACK!

I was so busy fighting off the Caners I didn't notice the shrubs with the strange flowers. Why were the flowers so strange? They had SHARP teeth! They were the GREEN BITERS!

CHOMP! CHOMP! CHOMP!

"Help!" I squeaked, grabbing my tail. I took off like a shot.

To my relief I ended up in what appeared to be a quiet clearing. Phew!

A moment later I felt something prick my paw. Rats! It was the Green Stingers!

The Green Stingers had long **POINTY** thorns.

STING! STING! STING!

Holey cheese, how do I always end up in the scariest places in the kingdom?! This forest was like no other. Not only were the plants alive, they all had **BAD ATTITUDES**! Oh, where was a good **plant counselor** when you needed one?

Right at that moment, the ground began to

s h a k e ...

Giant plants were galloping toward me. They were the ***GREEN RUSHERS***!

GALLOP! GALLOP! GALLOP!

I ran down the path, but a moment later I ended up with my snout **flat** on the ground!

The plants had stuck out their roots and had made me trip! They were the **GREEN TRIPPERS**!

KABONK!

I lay on the ground staring at the dirt. For a few minutes nothing happened. Was it over?

I sat up, feeling relieved . . . until suddenly, beneath my paws, a bunch of giant holes opened up! They were the Green Trappers, and they were trying to gobble me up!

GULP! GULP! GULP!

By some miracle, I managed to escape from the **GREEN FORESTS**. What a nightmare!

I sat on the path catching my breath. At that moment I noticed a patch of giant raspberries growing near me. They looked so **RED** and **JUICY** and delicious. My stomach grumbled. I was starving!

THE SEVEN GREEN FORESTS OF GREEN COUNTY

GREEN WHIPPERS

Are the best whippers in the kingdom. Stand back!

Ah!

Green Caners

Love to whack everyone with their thin branches. Youch!

Oww!

Help!

GREEN BITERS

Have flowers with supersharp teeth!

GREEN STINGERS

Use their thorns and spikes to sting everything in reach!

Ugh!

Green Rushers

Have powerful roots they use to gallop faster than a unicorn!

Shoo!

GREEN TRIPPERS

Rude and unpredictable, they love tripping those who least expect it!

Oops!

GREEN TRAPPERS

Capture, trap, and swallow . . . they are the most dangerous plants in the kingdom!

Argh!

I know they say you shouldn't eat berries in the **wild**, but I was so hungry. Maybe if I just tried a little one. Then, before I could pick anything . . .

You're Not a Tree!

hree chestnut trees yelled out, "**Stop right there!**"

"We know you're not a tree, you're a mouse!"

"Keep your paws off the **berries**!"

I gasped. "But who are you?" I squeaked. This place was getting nuttier by the minute. First the trees in the woods were out to get me and now three chestnut trees were screaming at me.

"We are the

the trees snarled. "We patrol the grounds of Green County."

"I promise I haven't done anything wrong!" I squeaked. "I was just minding my own business."

The Three Chestnut Trees

have powerful trunks and strong branches and are known as the legendary Chestnut Trees. They are legendary because long ago Mel the Magnificent used a magic de-rooting spell, which allowed the trees to pull up their roots from the ground. Now the three brothers can walk and even run!

The Three Chestnut Trees patrol all of Green County making sure everyone respects the Green Laws! Their names are Chester, Nutley, and Trunks Chestnut. The Chestnut Trees hail from the renowned Chestnut family. They provide Mel the Magnificent with the best chestnuts. They're his favorite snack!

CHESTER
CHESTNUT

NUTLEY
CHESTNUT

TRUNKS
CHESTNUT

The Three Chestnut Trees snorted, ELBOWING one another with their branches.

HA! HA! HA! HA! HA!

"Will you listen to this mouse? Minding his own business. What does he think, we were just germinated yesterday?!"

The first tree pinched my ear. "Listen, mouse, we heard you've already done a lot of damage since you entered the *Kingdom of Fantasy*. You can't fool us!"

The second tree yanked my tail. "We know you lost the Winged Ring. Even a seedling would know not to put it in a nightstand drawer!" he huffed.

Ouch!

The third tree stomped

on my paw. "Where did you put your garbage? Have you been littering the forest?!" he demanded.

The trees picked me up and shook me until some of my apples popped off.

"I'm not a littermouse!" I yelped.

"What about FIRES? Have you been lighting FIRES?" the trees snarled.

I shook my head. "I haven't lit a fire since I entered Green County, rodent's honor!"

"We saw how you looked at those **raspberries**. You looked ready to pick them!" they continued.

Uh-oh. They got me there. I had been drooling over those raspberries like a starving cat at a **fish festival**! "I'm sorry. I was really hungry," I apologized. "But I promise I didn't eat a thing!"

One of the chestnut trees lifted me up by my tail and swung me around until I was so **dizzy** I could hardly see the forest past the trees. "Sure,

Owwww!

sure. That's what they all say! 'Oh no, I didn't throw my garbage around! No, I didn't set any **FIRES**! No, I didn't eat any precious fruit!'" he mimicked.

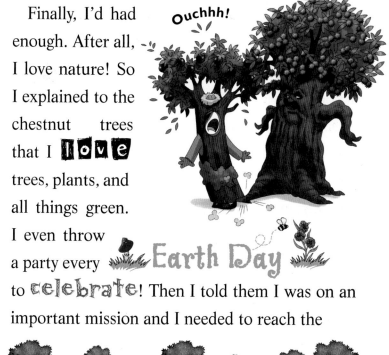
Finally, I'd had enough. After all, I love nature! So I explained to the chestnut trees that I **love** trees, plants, and all things green. I even throw a party every **Earth Day** to **celebrate**! Then I told them I was on an important mission and I needed to reach the

CIRCLE OF THE GREEN GUARDIANS,

The trees talked it over and agreed to let me continue on my way. However, they insisted on accompanying me. "This way we can make sure you don't do any damage to our grounds!"

And that was how, **accompanied** by the **Three Chestnut Trees**, I reached the

CIRCLE OF THE GREEN GUARDIANS.

The chestnut trees pushed me toward the Circle.
"Go on, from now on they will be the ones to set you straight!" they said.

One of them put a sack of **CANDIED CHESTNUTS** in my hand and told me, "When you get to

Mel the Magnificent,

bring him these candied chestnuts for us. Tell him the Three Chestnut Brothers send their regards! Got it?"

Another one shoved a **CANDIED CHESTNUT** in my mouth. "Not that you deserve it, but we want you to have a good, memory of us," he muttered.

I thanked the trees and approached the Guardians. I must admit I was a little distracted. That chestnut was **fabumouse**!

THE CIRCLE OF THE GREEN GUARDIANS

The Circle of the Green Guardians was made of a magic circle of

TWELVE OAK TREES.

These were ancient plants surrounded by an enchanted fog. Their trunks were gigantic, their branches knotted, and their leaves were thick and green.

Their leaves *rustled* in the wind in a peculiar way. I coughed. Either I was losing it, or those trees were WHISPERING to one another!

"Um, greetings, your leafy Lords, I mean, honorable BRANCH HANDS . . ." I sputtered.

THE CIRCLE OF THE GREEN GUARDIANS

They are alive and talk by rustling their leaves. During a full moon, they can transform into Wizards of Light. They were put at the edge of the Bright Empire by Mel the Magnificent to ensure that only the worthy could enter.

Here are their names:

Fronds Greenleaf: the most welcoming wizard

Oaky Woodthing: the most delicate wizard

Trunks Acornstrong: the strongest wizard

Barkabee Hardbark: the most severe wizard

Clorophyllis Greenbud: the liveliest wizard

Sapheart Bigleaf: the most generous wizard

Buddy Sweetleaf: the youngest wizard

Rooty Wellplanted: the wisest wizard

Oakland Barkster: the most decided wizard

Foliage Bloomsby: the greenest wizard

Treely Acornish: the oldest wizard

Leafly Happyblade: the happiest wizard

So much for making a good first impression! Oh, how were you supposed to address a **TALKING TREE** as tall as a ten-story building?

"I am dressed as a tree, but I'm actually a mouse," I continued. "They call me FOOLISH ONE, and **Blossom** sent me on a very important mission. So I, um, need to enter the

BRIGHT EMPIRE,

where Mel the Magnificent reigns. In fact, I really need to speak with him."

Suddenly, twelve voices whispered at once:

"If you want to enter the Bright Empire,
Step up now and show your desire.
We will let you pass (of this we're sure),
But only if your heart is pure.
We honor Blossom our noble protector,
We follow her rules and don't disrespect her."

I nodded impatiently. "Great, I understand, so can I go in?"

The oaks held out their branches.

Sparkle Flower

"Not so fast! You must take a test, before you can pass!"

Right then I remembered Sparkle Flower, the pendant of the secret alliance. I held it up, hoping the trees would skip the test and let me through.

Unfortunately, the plants just **shook** their leaves. "Sorry, mouse that will not do, you lost the ring, we can't trust you!"

At this I turned **red** as a tomato. What could I say? The oaks were right. Putting that ring in my nightstand drawer had ruined my reputation. No one trusted me anymore. Rats! But I didn't have time to dwell on my **MISTAKE** because the giant oaks began shooting questions at me.

"Before you take the test, tell us who you are."

"Why?"

"Because we need to know if you're a **witch**

or not!"

"I'm not a **witch**!"

This went on and on for twenty million hours. Well, okay, maybe they didn't question me for that long but you get the idea. Those oaks sure were suspicious! First they were convinced I was a witch, then they were certain I had witch relatives. Then they said I must be friends with witches.

At last, they handed me a **scroll**.

"Fill this out and that's all you need, If you pass, you may proceed." I took the scroll. Holey cheese, there were a lot of questions! This might take me all *day and night*! Using a goose feather and **BLUEBERRY JUICE** ink, I began jotting down my answers. I felt like I was back in school. Only, failing this test wouldn't just mean a bad grade. It would mean the end of **Queen Blossom**!

TEST
ARE YOU A FRIEND OF THE WITCHES?

1. WHAT CLOTHING DO YOU PREFER OUT OF THESE THREE:

A. A long dark dress, patent leather shoes, and a pointy hat

B. A black tunic with a black cape and a brooch shaped like a bat

C. A white tunic, a silver sword, and a magic wand made of an olive branch

2. WHICH COMPANION ANIMAL DO YOU PREFER?

A. A black cat that knows magic

B. A talking crow that knows how to say magic spells

C. A white dove that flies freely

3. WHAT WOULD YOU CHOOSE AS A TRANSPORTATION METHOD?

A. A flying broom

B. A black dragon that spits fire

C. A winged horse

4. WHAT WOULD YOU DO IF YOU FOUND YOURSELF IN A BEWITCHED FOREST AT NIGHT?

A. Gather nettle plants to stuff your pillow

B. Gather poisonous mushrooms and frog saliva to make a magic spell

C. Run in fright

5. IF YOU MET A WEREWOLF, YOU WOULD:

A. Share the latest gossip about the Kingdom of Witches

B. Ask for a tuft of its fur for a spell

C. Stay away

6. WHO WOULD YOU CHOOSE FOR A TRAVEL COMPANION?

A. A black dragon who loves plates of spicy peppers

B. A little ogre who loves fresh meat

C. A woodland gnome who loves desserts

TEST RESULTS

FRIEND OF THE FAIRIES

If you chose C for many of your answers then you are a loyal friend of the fairies. You love light, nature, and kindness. You have a good and affectionate heart and believe Blossom is the undisputed queen of all of the Kingdom of Fantasy!

FRIEND OF THE WITCHES

If you chose A or B for most of your answers, you are a friend of the witches. You love dark clothing, pointed hats, black cats, and bats. You like gathering poisonous mushrooms for potions and spells, and flying on a broom. You want Wither to reign over the Kingdom of Fantasy. Um, are you a witch by chance?

apple elm
magnolia cherry
chestnut
hawthorn cherry magnolia
sycamore olive chestnut pomegranate holly
sequoia poplar **poplar olive chestnut** pear
hawthorn cherry oak orange beech elm pear chestnut apple
apple mulberry linden sycamore birch elm linden
cherry oak orange beech elm spruce chestnut maple chestnut **spruce almond**
pine eucalyptus **magnolia elm** beech ash olive
magnolia almond cedar **pine** apple linden sycamore olive chestnut pine
fig pear hazlenut sequoia chestnut cedar **pear** fig
sequoia birch chestnut poplar orange **birch** mulberry pine orange hawthorn birch holly
fig **yew** magnolia **olive poppy** olive **chestnut** hawthorn cherry magnolia
magnolia cedar cherry elm hawthorn cherry magnolia birch holly sequoia elm pine
birch **magnolia** weeping willow maple **beech cypress** yew
birch magnolia **olive fig pear** cherry oak orange beech linden sycamore olive cypress
linden fig olive fig eucalyptus pear magnolia elm chestnut cherry elm
cherry magnolia chestnut cherry yew pear magnolia sequoia elm **magnolia cherry**
orange oak cherry birch pine mulberry eucalyptus magnolia
hawthorn fig olive cherry eucalyptus **sycamore olive chestnut pine**
sycamore birch cherry oak beech elm spruce chestnut
chestnut cherry eucalyptus birch magnolia pine
maple chestnut maple fig chestnut pear
cherry oak

How many names of trees make up the foliage of this tree?

Answer on page 573

TEST 3

HIDDEN FACES

Answer on page 574

How many faces can you see in this forest?

HUGGING A TREE

gave the oaks my test and waited. Not to brag, but I was feeling pretty **CONFIDENT**. After all, as **Aunt Ratsy** always says, "You can never go wrong if you tell the **truth**!"

Still, after a while I heard the Green Guardians muttering among themselves, "The mouse passed the exam. Do we let him through? How do we know his **HEART** is in the right place?"

My whiskers **drooped**. The oaks still didn't trust me. What else could I do? Give blood? Donate a lung?

Then I had an **IDEA**.

Spreading my paws as wide as I could, I

Sigh!

Hug a tree!

wrapped them firmly around the tree. Yep, you got it! I gave that tree the warmest *hug* ever! Suddenly, through the rough bark I could feel my mouse heart and the oak's heart **BEATING** together as if they were one. The sweetest feeling of FRIENDSHIP flowed through me, filling me up with a feeling of peace and joy.

The oak said, "Your heart is true, of this I'm sure, for it is beating, strong and pure."

Then all the other oaks stretched their branches toward me, singing,

"...Welcome, mouse, to the Bright Empire,
We hope you find what you desire,
Beyond the fog is a castle of gold,
And Mel the Wizard, of this we're told!..."

What a fabumouse castle!

I slipped out of my apple tree disguise and scampered off toward that enchanted fog.

I had arrived in the BRIGHT EMPIRE, the fabumouse kingdom governed by Mel the Magnificent, the Great Wizard of Light!

It wasn't long before a white-and-gold castle materialized before me. Wow! What a place! I took off running.

After all, time was ticking . . .

WOULD I MANAGE TO RETURN WITHIN ONE MOON CYCLE?

My heart HAMMERED under my fur as I pushed through the fog. At last, I reached the castle known as Sparkle Rock!

THE BRIGHT EMPIRE

Where it is told of how Foolish One was hit with a wand by Mel the Magnificent and received three magic gifts . . .

Sparkle Rock is a white castle with SPARKLING GOLDEN roofs and a flag with the crest of the BRIGHT EMPIRE on top.

THE HISTORY OF THE BRIGHT EMPIRE

It was founded in a secret time, in a secret way, with a secret formula made by the three most powerful wizards in the Kingdom of Fantasy: Mel the Magnificent, the Clever Chameleon, and the mysterious Lady of Dreams.

The three shared the same ideals for peace. They have fought together in a thousand battles, which has strengthened their friendship.

Queen Blossom joined the wizards in a hard-fought battle against the witches.

From that moment, the secret alliance was formed. It is made up of Blossom of the Flowers, Mel the Magnificent, the Lady of Dreams, and the Clever Chameleon.

THE MYSTERIOUS ANCESTRY OF WIZARDS

In the Kingdom of Fantasy there are fairies and witches, but there are also other magical creatures. The Wizards of Light live in an immense part of the kingdom beyond the enchanted mountains . . .

The wizards pass their time reading magic books and testing out spells. They are peaceful creatures and use their talents to combat the dark forces of evil. Besides spell and potions, they're not too bad at magic tricks, either!

The Bright Empire

CAPITAL: Sparkle Rock

RULER: Mel the Magnificent

CURRENCY: The Magical Wizzer

Magical Wizzers

MOTTO: Believe in magic!

GUARDIANS: The Green Guardians keep evil witches out of the kingdom.

AREA: No one knows how big it is because its borders are covered in bright, enchanted fog made of concentrated energy.

POPULATION: The Bright Empire is populated by many Magical Clans, including the Wizards of Light, and many kinds of enchanted animals.

SECURITY MEASURES:

The Wizards of Light have a unique power. They can become invisible at any time! In addition, the entire Bright Empire is invisible to anyone outside it. Only those chosen by the Green Guardians may enter. Mel the Magnificent came up with these special security measures to keep out evil powers. No witches allowed!

Coat of arms

THE BRIGHT EMPIRE ANTHEM

The Bright Empire welcomes you,
We believe in love that is pure and true.
May your thoughts be filled with warmth and virtue,
May sincerity shine in all that you do!

THE BRIGHT EMPIRE

1. Circle of the Green Guardians
2. Sparkle Rock Castle
3. Magic Rock Forest
4. Magical Observatory
5. Mystical Waterfall
6. Great Magic library
7. Wizardburg, where books are written
8. Harmonyville, the Land of Enchanted Elmdies
9. Wand Forest
10. Magic Market
11. Crystal Cavern
12. Mountain of Enchanted Snow
13. Wizardess Peak

14. Fountain of Truth

15. Pointed Hat Peak

16. Sincere Lake

17. Thicktail Castle
(Clan of the Foxes)

18. Sharptooth Castle
(Clan of the Wolves)

19. Great Claw Castle
(Clan of the Bears)

20. Clearwing Castle
(Clan of the Owls)

21. Von Wild Palace

22. Dreamreflector Lake

Anyone Home?

At the castle door there was a tall knight wearing **SPARKLY SILVER ARMOR**. When I got closer I realized that the armor was empty! It was a

PHANTOM KNIGHT!

The knight lowered his lance to block my way. "All right, then . . . Who are you? Where are you going? What do you want? Yada, yada, yada," he said in a dull voice. I guess it was boring asking the same questions over and over.

I cleared my throat. "I am FOOLISH ONE. I'm here to see Mel the Magnificent and —" I began.

"Why didn't you say so!" the knight interrupted, leaping aside to let me pass. "Come on in!"

SPARKLE ROCK CASTLE

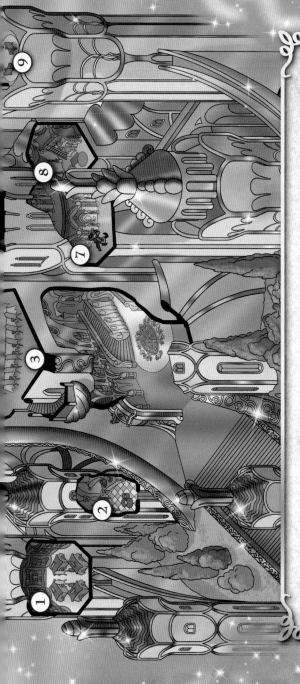

1. Mel's library
2. Kitchen
3. Banquet room
4. Mel's study (also converts to the Great Magic Council room)
5. Mirror room
6. Magic classroom
7. Gallery of ancient wizard portraits
8. Dormitory
9. Secret alliance room
10. Mel's apartment
11. The secret Magicarium room

The ghost knight pushed open the heavy door, and I entered the **magical castle**. I found myself in a large foyer with fancy **golden** arches.

I expected someone to greet me, but there was no one around. "Anyone home?" I yelled. No response. Something told me I should give up the idea of a

Welcome to My Castle Surprise Party.

Where is that music coming from?

At that moment I heard **Piano music** . . .

I decided to follow the music. I took a **candleholder** and began walking.

Cheese niblets! What a fright!

Along the corridor there were tens . . . hundreds . . . no thousands of **doors**. I'm not pulling your paw! The castle was one enormouse **maze**! I went from room to room following the music.

Suddenly, the music stopped and I heard sneezing:

Achoo! Achoo! Achoo!

I ran in its direction until I reached a room that was empty. There was no furniture, no books, no pictures . . . just an enormouse  MIRROR in a frame decorated with oak leaves and acorns. As I looked at the mirror, I got the impression that someone was looking at me. But I was alone in the room . . .

OR WAS I???

MEL THE MAGNIFICENT

 minute later, I heard another sneeze.

Achoo!

But still I didn't see anyone!

Then someone sneezed again.

Holey cheese balls, the sneezes were coming from the mirror!

Turns out that mirror opened just like a **DOOR**. On the other side there was another room, lit up by a candelabra on top of a

PIANO.

A man in a **FLOWING** white robe sat playing the piano. It was

Mel the Magnificent!

It's another room!

Mel stopped playing when he saw me. "Oh, ZIP and ZAP it, that's why I'm sneezing my face off! There's a mouse in the castle! I'm allergic to mice!"

He pointed a finger at me. "Is it possible to get just a **thousand** years' peace without someone coming to bother me? Oh well, since you're already here, talk, mouse."

Then he waved his WAND in the air. "But make sure you're telling the truth or I'll wand you!"

I hurried to explain, "I am here on a mission from our beloved Queen Blossom. She asked me to warn you, the Clever Chameleon, and the Lady of Dreams that her throne is in **DANGER**!"

The minute I mentioned **Blossom**, the Wizard brightened. "Oh, well, if you're here on behalf of my friend **Blossom** that's a different thing. How is my dear friend?" he asked.

Mel the Magnificent

SPARKLE FLOWER
the pendant of the secret alliance

MAGICARIUM
the book of magic

WANDRESS
the telescopic wand

Mel the Magnificent, the Great Wizard of Light, also known as Melvin, Wizard with the Wand, the Lord of Eternal Spells, the Protector of True Justice, and most of all, the Great Solver, He Who Is Able to Find a Solution Even When There Is None!

Mel's Story

Not much is known about Mel the Magnificent, and he's not talking! He lives alone, works alone, and prefers to be alone. (Too bad everyone is always asking him for help!) He is incredibly knowledgeable, and loves to read books and paint. He speaks all the languages of

Mel's ring

Wandress, Mel's magic wand

Magic tea and pastries

Mel's crown

Vial of magic water

the kingdom including Trollese, Witchish, Giantino, and Mermadian. He also knows the language of plants, the mysterious Green Language. He is the best musical composer in the Kingdom of Fantasy and wrote the "Anthem of the Bright Empire." He plays the piano, along with many other instruments. He is the greatest genius in all of the Kingdom of Fantasy and loves inventing bizarre machines. For example, he invented the Foggerator, a machine that makes Enchanted Fog. He uses his magic wand, known as Wandress, to protect the Bright Empire.

P.S. He is allergic to mice!

Magicarium, his personal book of magic

Mel's brush

Mel's favorite cookies

Silver inkwell with a goose feather

Magic glasses

I explained about Wither and the **STOLEN RING** and how Blossom might lose her title.

"What a disaster!" the wizard exclaimed. "Who was the **fool** who let the ring get stolen?"

Rats! I was hoping I wouldn't have to explain that part of the story. "Um, er, actually, it was me," I admitted.

Mel snorted. "Well, I can't say I'm surprised. You do have the look of a **fool**," he pointed out. Then he **JABBED** me with his elbow and smiled. "Okay, I'm just playing with you. I already know you lost the ring. I just wanted to see if you would tell the truth."

The wizard lifted his wand and a cloud of **SPARKS** shot out. "And now by my wizardly powers I hereby agree to help you in your quest to save our dear **queen** or my name isn't . . .

HOW TYPICAL!

Mel put his wand down and looked me in the eye. "Okay, let's hear it. What's the *big plan*? How are you going to fix the situation?" he asked.

I blinked. "Uh, well, I thought I would go to Wither, alone, and um, get the ring," I mumbled.

The wizard slapped his thigh. "Ha, ha, ha! Wow, what a CLEVER idea!" he hooted, rolling his eyes. "And tell me, how do you plan on surviving?"

"Er, um, I guess I was c-c-counting on you," I stammered.

Mel lifted his arms to the sky. "Well, of course you were! How typical! Everyone counts on me! 'Magnificent do this, Magnificent do that!' How is it possible that I am the only one who can fix anything in this kingdom?!"

Exasperated, he **smacked** his wand against the ground. "I'm telling you, I am fed up with all this helping out! Seriously, what about my problems? Who helps me out? Nobody, that's who!" he cried.

Uh-oh. The wizard was getting himself so RILED up I decided I'd better leave.

But when I turned, Mel **GRABBED** me by the tail.

"Who told you to leave?" he demanded.

I gulped.

"I said I was **fed up**, I didn't say I wouldn't help you!" he insisted. "Follow me!"

He headed toward the corner of the room and lifted a white veil that was covering . . .

AN ENORMOUSE TRANSPARENT CRYSTAL BALL!

"Check it out, mouse! With this magical crystal ball I can see everything that happens in the *Kingdom of Fantasy*, and more! And with this **powerful** ball I followed you during your whole trip. Just between us, I have never seen a more foolish rodent than you! How is it possible that you always get in so much trouble, FOOLISH ONE?"

This powerful ball of the purest crystal was personally made by Quartzy, the King of the Crystalline Gnomes. It allows you to see everything that happens in the Kingdom of Fantasy.

The Ball of Marvels

THE BALL OF MARVELS

Mel passed his hands over the CRYSTAL BALL, which immediately **lit up** light blue. "Okay, first things first," he mumbled. "Let's see how that ring got stolen. BALL OF MARVELS, show me Foolish One's house!"

Show me Foolish One's house!

The image of my house in **NEW MOUSE CITY** on Mouse Island appeared in the ball!

"Now, **BALL OF MARVELS**, show me inside Foolish One's house!" Mel continued.

The image changed and now you could see my kitchen. Then, to my embarrassment, I saw myself scarfing down different types of cheesy dishes. I remembered that day. I was trying out new **RECIPES**. "Yum! This is good!" I squeaked after each bite.

The wizard snickered as he continued to shout commands. "Ball, show me how the Winged Ring was **STOLEN**!"

I leaned in close. First, I saw myself going to sleep. Next, I saw the window open and a large **CROW** landing on my nightstand. With one wing he opened the drawer. Then he grabbed the ring in his beak and flew out the window.

The wizard grunted, "So that's how Wither did

it. She sent a crow! If only a CERTAIN SOMEONE hadn't put that ring in a certain place we wouldn't be in a certain mess."

I groaned. I mean, I felt awful, but how many times did a CERTAIN SOMEONE have to apologize?!

Mel rubbed the ball, and we watched as the crow delivered the ring to WITHER. It's hard to repeat what happened next. It was SO terrifying! The crow changed shape and transformed into a young warrior!

"Thank you, my betrothed! Now that I have the ring, my power will be unmatched! At last I will become the next **Queen of the Witches**!" Wither cackled.

Mel turned pale. "Oh boy. This is bad. That wasn't any crow, it was the Shape Shifter . . ."

The Shape Shifters
are creatures of the Kingdom of Fantasy that are capable of changing their form from human to animal.

CROWBAR THE CRUEL!

He pointed the WAND toward the ball, ordering, "Ball of Marvels, show me what WITHER is doing now!"

The magic ball showed Wither in the Kingdom of Witches. She was building a castle right in front of Cackle's that was taller, **SCARIER**, and DARKER than hers!

She danced and sang a mysterious song . . .

Here's what I saw in the

1

I saw my house in New Mouse City.

2

I was testing out recipes.

5

He flew out the window . . .

6

And brought the ring to Wither.

Ball of Marvels · · ·

3

I went to bed, and a large crow flew in the window.

4

He took the winged ring.

7

It was no ordinary crow, it was Crowbar the Cruel!

8

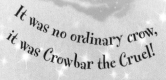

Then I saw Wither building a really tall castle.

Wither's Castle

Wither of the Flowers

"In the name of Wither,
I will build a castle,
I will build it before dawn,
It will be no hassle,
I will use my magic,
To put things together,
I will make it dark and strong,
To withstand deadly weather,
Tall and dark and super scary,
And definitely haunted,
With my picture on the walls,
Hey, I've got it, I can flaunt it!
I want it tall, I want it big,
I want it worthy of a queen,
I want it facing the west wind . . .
So I'm the first one to be seen.
Oh, and one more little thing,
and then that's all there is,
I need a magical assistant,
to handle all my biz!"

Then the witch waved her wand in the air, and a **BLACK CAT** appeared. It had yellow eyes, really long whiskers, and an ear-piercing *Meowww*!

Wither smiled evilly. "I have the **RING**, I have the castle . . . and now I have the assistant,

THE **MENACE, CHATTERING CAT**."

What a feline fright!

Twisted rattails! The cat looked as **EVIL** as its boss!

Mel turned off the CRYSTAL BALL with a wave of his wand. "Well, that's that. You've made a real mess of things, FOOLISH ONE. The only way to fix it is to go to

and get the Winged Ring back from Wither. If you're lucky, you'll make it back alive," he said with a sigh.

"G-go to Dark Castle?" I stammered. "Couldn't I try c-c-c-calling first or maybe sending an email or t-t-text?"

The wizard snorted. "Couldn't I send a text?!" he shrieked, imitating me. "Foolish One, your FOOLISHNESS astounds me! I can't . . ."

He was interrupted by *a terrible noise*.

SIIIILENCE!

el slipped *Wandress* under his arm and turned, motioning me to follow.

He headed toward one wing of the castle where there was a **SIGN** in Fantasian.*

We headed quickly down a hallway. On the way, we passed many doors with many signs hanging from them: Spell Room, Magic Laboratory,

Professor's Lounge, Wizard Gym, Magic Library, Enchanted Cafeteria.

"Welcome to the School for Wizards! All that racket is coming from the first-year students," Mel explained. "It's a really undisciplined class. But I'll set things straight. What else is new?

to the rescue!"

There were pictures with class portraits along the walls. I rubbed my eyes, thinking I was dreaming . . .

Cheese and crackers!
The wizards in the pictures
were moving! They were enchanted!

SCHOOL FOR WIZARDS
FIRST YEARS

Mel stopped in front of the door to a classroom that read First Years — Beginner Wizards on it.

He **flung** open the door and yelled,

"SILENCE!"

There was total chaos in the classroom.

One wizard was making **pizzas**.

Pizza for everyone!

Another was playing with **balls** of magic light.

In one corner three wizards were trying new and wacky **HAIRDOS**.

248

A little wizard with **red** hair was drawing a funny picture of Mel on the chalkboard.

Everyone was yelling and laughing and running around.

As soon as the class saw Mel they sprang into a WHIRLWIND of frenzied action.

A few minutes later everyone was seated quietly in their places with innocent looks plastered on their faces.

Mel walked over to the picture on the board and looked it over carefully. "For those of you who don't know, IRRESPONSIBLE is spelled with an 'i' not an 'a,'" he observed dryly.

Then with a wave of his MAGIC WAND he fixed the spelling and erased the drawing of himself. He replaced it with a much more serious self-portrait.

With a second wave of his wand he took all of the little wizards' wands and slipped them in a drawer of the desk. Zap! With a third wave of his wand a list of the Seven Magic Laws appeared on the board. "Copy these ten, no, one hundred, no one thousand times, and then (if you're lucky) I will give your wands back!" Mel ordered.

The Magic Laws

1) A real wizard seeks out the good and avoids the bad.

2) A real wizard behaves their best, because with great power comes great responsibility.

3) A real wizard tells the truth.

4) A real wizard uses magic for good and noble reasons.

5) A real wizard uses magic only when necessary.

6) A real wizard keeps their wand in a safe place.

7) A real wizard never wastes their powers on silly spells.

RECOGNIZE ME?

Right then a little wizard who had been working QUIETLY at her desk stood up. "It's not fair! I didn't do anything wrong! Why am I in trouble?!" she protested.

"But that's just it, Wolfy!" Mel declared. "You didn't do anything! You should have stopped the rest of the class. You will do the ASSIGNMENT just like everyone else. No special treatment here."

The little wizard rolled her eyes. "What else is new, Uncle," she muttered.

Mel turned to me and said, "Foolish One, meet my niece, **Wolfy**."

Wolfy seemed like a strange name for a wizard, but I'm not exactly an expert on wizard names.

Wolfy

She comes from the mythical Magic Wolf Clan, wizards who can transform into wolves. She is Mel's niece and the smartest in her class. She likes to brag that she knows all the spells by heart. Too bad her overconfidence often gets her in trouble.

"It's an honor to meet you," Wolfy said, politely shaking my paw. "I know everyone calls you Foolish One, but my friends and I have been following your adventures. To me, you will always be the Prince."

One by one Wolfy's friends stepped up to shake my paw.

ROXY FOXY

Owlivia

BEARTINA

Roxy Foxy

She comes from the mythical Magic Fox Clan, wizards who can turn into foxes. Roxy has a passion for fashion. She knows how to make invisible cloaks and enchanted hats and is the guardian of her clan's treasure: scissors, a needle, and thread.

Beartina

She comes from the mythical Magic Bear Clan,
wizards who can turn into bears. She is strong
and athletic and knows how to heal bodies
and spirits thanks to her knowledge of herbal
medicine. Her specialty? Herbal teas!

Owlivia

She comes from the mythical Magic Owl Clan, wizards who can turn into owls. She is very courageous and knows how to fly and shoot a bow and arrow. She has a passion for magic jewels and wears a pendant in the shape of an owl's head around her neck.

The wizard Owlivia was the last to introduce herself. I couldn't put my paw on it, but she seemed so familiar. Was it her twinkling eyes? Her curious expression? The familiar-looking pendant in the shape of an owl she wore around her neck?

Where had I seen them before?

"Don't you recognize me, Prince?" she said with a wink. "We've already met."

Before I could say "squeak," she suddenly began to twirl in a circle *faster* and *faster* and *faster*

until . . . she transformed into a !

Now I knew where I had seen Owlivia before. She was the enormouse white owl who had flown me from Mouse Island to the Kingdom of Fantasy!

"You might want to file your **PAWNAILS**, Prince," she remarked. "You were holding on so tight on the trip over I lost a ton of feathers."

I blushed.

OH, HOW EMBARRASSING!

Hello, Prince!

Whoa!

WHERE'S MY THRONE?!

Satisfied that the young **wizards** were once again working hard, Mel led me back to his study. "Okay, so where was I before I was so **RUDELY** interrupted?" he griped. "Ah, yes, I was about to help you save Blossom. So first things first, I will summon the

Great Magic Council!"

He pulled a white velvet string that was tied to a **GOLDEN BELL**. "Wizards of the Bright Empire, look alive! The Council of Wizards is now in session!" he cried.

Then he waved his wand in the air singing, "Wider, bigger, make more space! Brighten up this small dark place!"

book of spells
wizard book of spells
magic wand book of spells
wizard magic magic wand book of spells
marvel wonder wizard magic magic wand crystal ball book of spells
magic spell magic marvel wonder wizard magic magic
magic spell magic formula wizard
magic spell magic marvel wonder wizard magic
magic wand magic wand
magic spell magic marvel
magic spell magic marvel wonder wizard magic wand crystal ball book of spells wizard hat magic
magic spell magic marvel wonder wizard magic magic wand crystal ball book of spells wizard
wand crystal ball
wizard magic magic wand bo
magic wand crystal ball book of s
magic formula magic
crystal ball
wizard

Then he began to twirl around and around so fast, just watching him was making me **dizzy**! As he spun, the room seemed to grow **bigger** and **bigger**. Cheese rinds! Were my eyes playing tricks on me?

Finally, the wizard stopped **spinning** and waved his wand in the air with a flourish. "That's it! The room is big enough. And now for some furniture!" In a loud voice he began to sing, "One, two, three, four, chairs and tables,

One, two, three . . .

lamps and more! Five, six, seven, eight, my books and bookshelves would be great!"

The walls filled up with shelves that had books of all kinds on them.

So this was the wizard's famous

magical
Library!

Legend had it, Mel's library contained the most precious books of spells in all of the *Kingdom of Fantasy*!

With another wave of the wand, Mel conjured up heavy gold-embroidered silk curtains for the windows. And when he pointed the WAND toward the floor, expensive $decorative$ rugs appeared. Then he yelled, "I'm still waiting for those chairs! And soft pillows, pairs and pairs!"

A **TORNADO** of chairs in all kinds of fabrics and styles swirled into the room. Pillows round and square, many with **gold tassels**, rained down, too.

Youch!

The wizard looked around, nodding in approval until his expression clouded over. "Oh, zap it! Where's my throne? I need my throne!" he screeched.

Suddenly, a super-heavy **throne** dropped right on my paw!

Youchhhhhhhhhhhhh!

"Do you mind getting your paw out from **under** my throne?" Mel huffed.

Ow!

Aiyee!

I was about to protest when he ordered, "Have a seat."

Right then a **STOOL** landed on my other paw.

"Ow!" I squeaked.

Mel shook his head. "You really are a FOOLISH ONE," he commented. "Here, have some tea and pastries."

Without warning, a tea kettle crashed down, **sloshing** hot tea on my tail.

"Aiyee!" I yelped.

"Seriously, mouse? Can you go two seconds without getting into trouble? Here, sit down next to me so I can keep my eye on you," the wizard ordered.

Then he held a hand to his ear. "**LISTEN**, mouse, they're coming!"

I put my paw to my own ear but I have to say I heard nothing, nada, zip.

"Let's go, let's go, let's go!" the wizard commanded. "I don't have all day here!"

I was beginning to think the wizard had lost a few **marbles** when I heard the sound of *feet running*. How strange. There was no one in sight!

Listen, mouse, they're coming!

LOOK AT ALL
THE WIZARDS!

el noticed my puzzled expression and whipped out a pair of **TRIANGULAR** glasses. "Here, take these, mouse. They're **ENCHANTED GLASSES** that will allow you to see everything," he explained.

As soon as I placed the glasses on my nose the whole room came into focus. I could see thousands of **wizards** hurrying around.

Ooohhh!

"Hurry, hurry!" they whispered to one another. "Take your seats. Mel the Magnificent is about to speak!"

"I have called you here on an

important matter," Mel announced. "But first I made everyone . . . wait for it . . . **Magic Cookies!**"

The room went crazy. Apparently, Mel's Magic Cookies were a crowd favorite. I took a nibble. Tasty, yes, but nothing compared to my **chocolate cheesy chews**. (Shhh! Don't tell the wizard!)

After the wizards had eaten, Mel got down to business. "Time to

THINK... THINK... THINK... THINK... THINK... THINK... THINK... THINK... THINK... THINK... THINK... THINK... THINK... THINK...

We need to find a way to help Foolish One so we can save Blossom!" he said.

Answer on page 574

Can you find the one wizard holding a guitar?

Wizard Council of the Bright Empire

Somer and Sault
Wizard professors of
magic gymnastics

Brush and Floss
Wizard dentists

Flora and Fauna
Wizards of natural secrets

Simmer and Sauté
Wizard cooks

Rhyme and Reason
Wizard advisors

Dewey and Decimal
Wizard librarians

Jewel and Gem
Wizard jewelers

Primsy and Proper
Wizards of etiquette

Leap and Twirl
Wizards of dance

Scribbles and Wordsy
Wizard scribes

Hot and Cold
Wizard meteorologists

Brick and Cement
Wizard architects

Show and Tell
Wizard interpreters

Spray and Sniff
Wizard perfumers

Hue and Palette
Wizard painters

Divide and Multiply
Wizard accountants

Hemmy and Stitch
Wizard tailors

Selfie the wizard
A wanderer who travels
alone through the
Kingdom of Fantasy

Seek and Find
Wizard explorers

Maybe and Perhaps
Indecisive wizards

Giggles and Riddles
Wizard joke makers

Harmonia and Tuner
Wizard music teachers

WHERE ARE HIS MUSCLES?

The wizards leaned forward as Mel laid out the whole sorry story. He explained about **WITHER** and **CROWBAR THE CRUEL** and the stolen Winged Ring and blah, blah, blah. It all added up to bad news for Blossom!

Who was the fool?

How could he?

What a scatterbrain!

As soon as Mel mentioned the ring, the wizards all began to complain. "Who was the FOOL who failed to protect the ring?"

"How could he be so careless?"

"What a scatterbrain!"

"Ahem, yes, what a simpleton," I chimed in, hoping no one would realize I was the one they were complaining about.

Too bad Mel ratted me out. "It was him!" he said, pointing.

The whole room turned to glare at me. Oh, where was a good disappearing spell when you needed one?!

"We're in trouble," Mel continued. "Wither is calling for a

NEW QUEEN

to be elected . . . and we all know who she'll be voting for . . . her wicked self! We need to help the mouse reach the **Kingdom of Witches** and retrieve that ring."

Everyone looked at me doubtfully.

"Him? We're sending a cheese-chomping mouse to the Kingdom of Witches?"

"He'll never make it back alive!"

"Where are his **MUSCLES**?"

"What are his magic powers?"

Mel nodded in agreement. "He is a puny thing, and to top it off, he has no **magic powers**.

But there must be some way we can help him in the name of our queen, Blossom."

Wither's safe

Mel waved his hand over the **BALL OF MARVELS**. Before long a picture appeared. It showed a huge **golden** safe wrapped in heavy metal chains. "Looks like this is where Wither keeps the Winged Ring. She put it in the **WICKED SAFE**, the safest safe in the Kingdom of Witches."

With the magic wand he made an *enchanted key* appear.

"Take this, mouse, and be careful not to lose it. This is *Open-up, the Enchanted Key*. It opens everything, and I mean everything — all the locks in the Kingdom of Fantasy, including the **WICKED SAFE**!"

Mel peered once more at the ball. "It will be tricky to get into Dark Castle, so I'd better give you a disguise. I can make you a **DARK KNIGHT** or a **wicked wizard** or an **EVIL HUNTSMAN**," he said.

Then he looked me up and down. "No, I've got it, I'll dress you like a

GOOFY OGRE!"

Again Mel studied the ball. "The trip will be long and difficult. Wither has lots of allies all over the Kingdom. I'd better give you my personal dragon,

LIGHTBRIGHT, DRAGON OF FORTUNE.

Just bring him back without a single scratch, got it?"

Open-up,
The Enchanted Key!

I am Open-up,
I am a magic key.
I can open any lock,
Metal, brick, stone, or rock.
I work only for the good,
And in every neighborhood.
But put me down if you are bad,
I'll burn your hand
and make you mad!

Open-up is a magic key that opens all locks
in the Kingdom of Fantasy. It was created by
Wizard Molten Rock and can do its job only if
it is in the hands of those who are acting with
good intentions. If one has bad intentions, the
key will burn their hand.

The Goofy
OGRE DISGUISE

mushrooms
in the ears

long yellow
fingernails

rotten moss
hair

curly
nose
hair

woven algae
clothing

The Goofy Ogres are very small and very
stinky. Instead of hair they have rotten moss on
their heads, and poisonous mushrooms growing
in their ears! Their nails are long and yellow
and covered in mold. They wear clothes woven
from swamp algae, take showers in vulture pee,
and grease their hair with drool!

Lightbright, the Dragon of Fortune

*I fly faster than
the strongest breeze,
When my heart is
happy I'm well at ease!
The wizard is my
generous keeper,
With his love my
strength grows deeper.*

He is made up of the light of stars and has extraordinary strength. His feet kick the strongest blows, his tail can wipe out any enemy, and he breathes a deadly ray of light. His eyes are the purest stars, and along his spine seven stars shine. But the most extraordinary star is his heart: He is incredibly loyal to his owner, Mel the Magnificent.

A STINKY DISGUISE

I couldn't wait to see Lightbright, the Dragon of Fortune. A dragon made up of twinkling stars sounded magical. Unfortunately, I had to wait for the sun to go down for the official meet and greet. It seemed LIGHTBRIGHT was awake only at night because he fed on starlight!

The wizard raised his wand and prepared to conjure up my ogre disguise.

Couldn't I just dress like a wizard?

"Any way you could make me a friendly wizard costume instead?" I asked.

"Must I spell everything out for you, Foolish One?" Mel huffed. "If you show up at Dark Castle dressed in a friendly white wizard costume, Wither will think you are from the BRIGHT EMPIRE. She'll feed you to Menace, the Chattering Cat!

Then he said,

"Give me vulture pee
And soap from bat poop,
Stinkyfool drool,
And flies thick as soup!"

Tub of vulture pee . . .

Soap made from bat poop . . .

Stinkyfool drool . . .

Tons of flies!

289

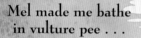

He dressed me in clothes
made of algae . . .

He covered me in a
cloud of flies . . .

Finally, he said, "I challenge anyone to
figure out that you're not a real ogre!"

WHAT ARE YOU DOING HERE?

s soon as I was disguised as an ogre, I looked in the mirror and let out a scream. "Aaaargh!"

I was truly horrible-looking!

And I was so stinky!

I was trying my hardest not to gag when the door to the Great Magic Council room flew open and a young wizard strode in. It was Wolfy, Mel's niece!

"Niece, what are you doing here? You are not allowed into the Great Magic Council yet! You are still an **apprentice**!" Mel the Magnificent shrieked.

WOLFY

Come here, bottle!

I know what you're thinking!

I want a cake!

Wolfy is the daughter of Howler, the King of the Wolves, of the Magic Wolf Clan; and of Melissa, Mel's sister, of the Bright Wizard Clan. She has two amazing gifts, the power of the Wolf Clan (the ability to transform into a wolf) and the power of the Bright Ones (the ability to perform magic). Even as a child, Wolfy has been able to turn into a wolf, move objects, read minds, and perform spells. She is bright and stubborn just like her uncle!

Wolfy marched up to her uncle. "I am volunteering to accompany this mouse to Dark Castle. He has **no chance** on his own," she said.

"And you have **no chance** of going!" Mel responded. "You haven't finished your apprenticeship! It's way too

DANGEROUS!

I said no!

Huff · · ·

Wolfy **stamped** her foot. She was the smartest wizard in her class, and her uncle knew it. It wasn't fair that he always treated her like a baby. Then she had an idea. "Why don't you test me, Uncle, to see if I am ready?" she suggested.

Reluctantly, Mel agreed. He would give his niece three E X A M S that only real wizards would know how to pass. "Ready?" Mel asked.

"Of course!" Wolfy responded confidently.

For her first test, Mel **LAUNCHED** three apples into the air, one after the other. "Show me that you know how to use your wand with precision," he said. "Let's see how many apples you can hit."

Wolfy waved her WAND and struck the three apples in just one shot! The **APPLES** were surrounded by a blue light and fell to the ground. A second later they transformed into a delicious-smelling apple cake!

Everyone exclaimed, "**OOOOOOH!**"

FIRST TEST:
Precision spells!

Zap!

With another touch of her wand, Wolfy covered the cake with whipped cream and powdered cinnamon.

"AAAAAAH!" the crowd exclaimed.

Then with another touch of her magic wand, she cut the cake into pieces and served it to everyone on little silver plates. Once again everyone cheered, "OOOOOOH!"

Mel tasted the cake and **LICKED** his lips. "Not bad! Now show me that you know how to complete a Transformation spell."

Mel pointed at me. "Turn

that mouse . . . into a **mosquito**!" he ordered.

Wolfy took her wand and pointed it at me. I didn't even have time to say "squeak" before I was transformed into a mosquito!

"WHOA!" everyone exclaimed in admiration.

I, on the other paw, flew all around, buzzing frantically,

Thankfully, Mel ordered that Wolfy turn me back into a mouse, and that

Zap!

spell worked, too! **WHEW!**

Mel scratched his head. He knew Wolfy was good, but he hadn't realized she was this good.

What a surprise . . . surprise . . . surprise . . . surprise . . .

SECOND TEST:
Transformation spell!

Zap!

Squeeeak!

That's me! Transformed into a mosquito! Heeeeelp!

Finally, Mel said, "Show me that you know how to tame a

Storm Dragon."

He whistled and a Storm Dragon appeared at the window. They are the wildest dragons in the Kingdom of Fantasy!

SECOND TEST:
Retransformation spell!

Zap!

Wolfy approached the dragon's face as it huffed

BOILING VAPORS.

Holey Swiss slices! What a scary sight! One flaming puff from that dragon and the little wizard would be toast!

Wolfy didn't flinch. Instead she let the humongous Storm Dragon sniff her hand. Then

THIRD TEST:
Tame a Storm Dragon!

Can I have a ride?

she began to scratch him behind the right ear. "**OOOO!**" crooned the dragon happily. Next Wolfy scratched behind his left ear. "**AHH!**" The dragon sighed, closing his eyes.

The little wizard smiled. "Will you take me for a ride?" she asked the dragon.

The dragon hesitated, but when Wolfy offered to scratch his ears while they were flying, he grinned. Then the dragon lowered his head, and Wolfy jumped on his back. They took off into the sky.

All the wizards ran to the window to watch them.

"**WOW!**" they cried as Wolfy had the dragon do a few loop-the-loops.

NOT RANGER!

ell, Uncle, I passed your tests!" Wolfy said proudly, climbing off the Storm Dragon.

Mel the Magnificent nodded. He had to admit, the kid was pretty **good**. Still, she was only a kid. "Okay, you can go," he agreed. "But **Ranger the Ghost Guardian,** is going with you."

"**Not Ranger!**" Wolfy whined. "He won't let me do anything fun!"

"That's exactly why I chose him," Mel explained. "You need someone who can keep an eye on you! Take it or leave it!"

Of course, Wolfy agreed. What choice did she have?

RANGER THE GHOST GUARDIAN

This strange silver armor behaves like a real knight (he even knows how to watch Sparkle Rock, Mel's castle!) but he is completely empty inside! Before Mel found him, Ranger was a rental costume in a Halloween party store. His big dream was to one day become a real knight who went on real adventures.

Mel, who sees and knows everything, found the armor and named him Ranger. He made him the Ghost Guardian of the Bright Empire. Now Ranger spends his days at Sparkle Rock defending it from intruders.

Ranger takes his job seriously but does find it a little boring. Most of his days are spent questioning visitors at the castle door. Ho hum. He is big on appearances and spends a lot of time shining his armor.

Then Mel clapped his hands and we heard the sound of clanking armor.

Ranger, the Ghost Guardian, clink, clank, clunked into the room. I recognized him. He was the knight from the front of the castle.

"Hello again," I said, sticking out my paw to shake his hand.

"No time for chitchat, mouse," Mel interrupted. "Everyone, listen up!

The Great Witch Council

will start tomorrow at midnight. That means Foolish One, Ranger, and Wolfy, you need to leave immediately. LIGHTBRIGHT, the Dragon of Fortune, will take you to Dark Castle. But remember, you need to finish your trip before daybreak. **LIGHTBRIGHT** will vanish at the first **RAYS** of the sun."

Wolfy beamed. "Thanks, Uncle! I always wanted to ride **LIGHTBRIGHT**. I'll take good care of him. And don't worry, I've got this all under control. I already mapped out the route so that we will arrive before the **SUN** rises. Piece of cake!" she said confidently.

I was glad someone was confident. The idea of going to **Dark Castle** on such a scary mission filled me with dread. Still, like it or not . . .

THE ADVENTURE WAS ABOUT TO BEGIN!

TWO SPY HATS

I followed everyone out of the room on shaky paws. Oh, what had I gotten myself into this time? Then again, at least I didn't have to go to the witches' kingdom all alone.

Wolfy waved me off when I tried to thank her. "It's nothing," she said. "This will show Uncle Mel I'm not a **little** girl anymore! Are you ready? We'll leave right after

SUNSET."

I followed Wolfy to the wizard dormitories. Inside the room, Wolfy's friends Owlivia, ROXY FOXY, and BEARTINA were super-excited.

"You were great, Wolfy!" Owlivia exclaimed.

"Congrats!" Roxy added.

"Was it hard to transform Foolish One back from a **mosquito** to a mouse?" Beartina asked.

"It was almost impossible!" Wolfy admitted. "For a while I was afraid he'd have to remain a **mosquito** forever!"

Stars swam before my eyes. I pictured myself as a mosquito, buzzing around for the rest of my life. What a total nightmare! I would lose my fur and I would have to live on blood. BLECH! Plus, how would I communicate with my friends and family? I was glad I didn't have to find out!

I was still thinking about **mosquitos** when Roxy said, "We have a GIFT for you, Wolfy. Two spy hats!"

"You'll wear one and you'll give the other to

Wither," Owlivia explained. She held out two pointy witch hats. Each one was decorated with an enormouse sparkly **RUBY** in the middle.

The friends plunked one of the witch hats on Wolfy's head. Beartina placed the other hat carefully in a solid-gold hatbox with the Fantasian letters WOTF* etched into it (they were the initials of Wither of the Flowers).

Then the three friends sang:

♫ "A HAT FOR YOU AND THE WITCH, TOO,
IT'S MADE OF MAGIC, JUST FOR YOU,
PUT IT ON AND YOU WILL KNOW,
SECRETS TOLD BOTH HIGH AND LOW!"

Wolfy tapped the hat on her head with tears in her eyes. "Aw, you guys are the best. I mean it, what would I do without you?" she cried. Then she hugged her friends happily.

Wolfy had never heard of a spy hat so her friends explained what it could do. Apparently,

*You will find the Fantasian alphabet on page 571.

when Wither put the hat on her head, it would communicate with Wolfy's hat. "This way you can find out where the **SAFE** is hidden!" explained Roxy.

Then the three friends pointed their MAGIC WANDS at the hats.

They sang:

"THESE HATS WILL WORK AS A PAIR,
AND EVERY IMAGE WILL BE SHARED!
WHAT ONE SEES THE OTHER SEES, TOO,
SO WOLFY WILL KNOW WHAT TO DO!"

The two spy hats **shimmered**. They looked so cool I began to feel drab and ridiculous in my **GOOFY OGRE DISGUISE**. Ah, well. As my great-grandma Ratsy always told me, "The clothes don't make the mouse!"

Anyway, where was I? Oh yes, the four friends united their wands and sang,

"We promise on our
magic wands,
Our friendship is made
of the thickest bonds!"

INSTRUCTION MANUAL

The hat charges when it is exposed to moonlight.

BLACK PEARL:
the hat's switch

RUBY:
used to control the volume of the transmission of information

Hat #1

This hat observes and listens to everything Wither says and does. The hat then transmits the information to the second hat, which Wolfy wears. How did the three wizards make the Spy Hat? With a powerful magic spell!

FOR THE TWO SPY HATS!

BLACK PEARL:
the hat's switch

PEACOCK FEATHER:
moving it works like an antenna

RUBY:
serves to control the volume of the reception of information

Hat #2

This hat receives all the information from the first hat and tells Wolfy everything Wither does!

To turn it on, just turn the black pearl at the top of the hat. To turn it off, just pull the same black pearl two times.

THE SEVEN VON WILD BROTHERS

"This trip will be **DANGEROUS**, but I'm ready. How about you, Prince?" Wolfy asked.

I gulped. What if . . .

Wither locked me up . . .

Or turned me into a toad . . .

Or fed me to her cat?!

With my whiskers **trembling** in **fright** I stammered, "Well, um, I g-g-g-guess. B-b-but if we got in t-t-trouble we could ask Mel for help, right?"

Wolfy frowned. "We won't need help! Not from my uncle!" she insisted. "But if we did I'd just call

the Seven VON WILD Brothers."

"Ah, the Von Wild brothers," Roxy murmured. "They're so strong and powerful and nice, and they're also very CUTE."

It was then that the door opened and the VON WILD brothers entered.

The Seven
VON WILD
Brothers

BLOWER
the power of wind

STRIKER
the power of lightning

Clinker
the power of ice

The seven Von Wild brothers are the children of Storm and Sunshine, the Wizards of the atmospheric elements. Each one of them possesses a great power. They live together in a flying palace shaped like a dragon.

FOGGER
the power of fog

Hailer
the power of hail

RAINER
the power of rain

BOOMER
the power of thunder

The Flying Palace

Ray holder stores the moon rays that are transformed into energy.

Rudder steers palace.

Copper heaters are warmed by the sun.

Mechanical wings use mirrors to capture the sun's energy.

Propeller motor

Wizard meeting hall

The Flying Palace is the only land in the Kingdom of Fantasy that has no borders, but is made up exclusively of a Flying Palace.

The seven young wizards entered the room. Each wizard put his hand over his heart and yelled his name.

FOGGER STRIKER Clinker BOOMER RAINER Hailer BLOWER

The oldest one spoke up. "Foolish One, you are our favorite hero! Even if you messed up by allowing the ring to be stolen, you can count on the seven Von Wild brothers!"

Wolfy smiled. "You see, Prince! The Von Wild brothers can be our backup. They can turn into **DRAGONS**, and they have the power of the elements."

Right then one of the brothers' cell phones began to buzz.

BUZZ! BUZZ! BUZZ!!

Who knew wizards had cell phones?

"We need to go!" Striker cried. "Our break is over. Professors Seek and **Find*** do not tolerate lateness! Last time we were late they made us recopy the map of the *Kingdom of Fantasy* thirty times!"

Then they ran out of the room as quick as **LIGHTNING**.

"Let's find the perfect **witch disguise** for Wolfy to wear to Dark Castle," said Roxy. She pulled out a huge chest filled with costumes.

I saw a clown's wig, a **fuzzy** bear suit, and even a cat costume! How scary!

Wolfy's witch look

A black dress as dark as the dead of night

Snake bracelets and pointy boots

Then Wolfy got dressed in her witch costume and I fainted with fear! Squeeaaak!

She looked exactly like a

Witch!

Squeak!
How scary!

She put on the witch costume and I fainted in fright!

THE MAGIC
MAGICARIUM

Wolfy **WAVED** her wand over my head and I came to.

"Seriously, Prince? Does this seem like the time to **FAINT**?" she grumbled. "I hope you're not going to pass out when we see the real witches."

Does this seem like the time to faint?

Ouchie!

So much for sympathy. Wolfy was just like her uncle Mel.

"Well, um, it's only because I wasn't expecting it. When we are at **Dark Castle** I won't **faint**, I mean, I'll do my best, well I'll give it my best shot . . ." I muttered. Did I mention I'm not the **BRAVEST** mouse? Okay, let's face it, I'm a certified scaredy-mouse!

Just then I looked out the window. The sun was about to set. There was no time to worry about **WITCHES** — it was almost time to go! I checked that Open-up, the key, was in my bag, took the **GOLD HATBOX** and Wolfy's luggage, and followed the **wizard** down the hall.

RANGER, THE GHOST GUARDIAN, led the way as we crossed through big rooms and small rooms, SMALLER rooms and **BIGGER** rooms, up the stairs and down the stairs, and down the stairs and up the stairs, and then up, up, up, up, up until we reached a **GOLDEN DOOR** that had Fantasian* writing on it:

You will find the Fantasian alphabet on page 571.

囗 ↯ ⊙ ⊤ ⵑ ↯ ▱⊙⊤ ⓜ 囗
▱⊙ 𝟖 𝟖 囗

Wolfy pushed the door and went in. She pointed to a large book open on a lectern.

"That is the Magicarium. Maybe one day my uncle Mel will let me use it. It contains everything really useful that a wizard needs to know," she said.

Then she touched the cover gently and, as if by some spell, the pages RUSTLED and turned on their own . . .

Flip Flip Flip Flip Flip Flip Flip Flip Flip Flip Flip Flip

Next, Wolfy told me the STORY of the Magicarium . . .

The Magicarium

The Magicarium is Mel the Magnificent's personal book of magic.

He is a talking book and is Mel's most trusted advisor. He is also the only one in the kingdom who can handle Mel's stubborn attitude!

His pages were written by hand with enchanted ink by Bulber the Great, the founder of the magical dynasty of the Bright Wizards. They were written on a scroll that came from the rare Glowbulbous plant, which only blooms every hundred years on Mount Shiner on the night of the first full moon of summer.

The Magicarium is a book with immense power. In the hands of the wrong person the book could become extremely dangerous . . . So Mel keeps him in a secret room.

The Magicarium dreams of living new adventures with new friends and using his power to fight witches. That's why he decides to follow Wolfy and Foolish One on their adventure.

LIGHTBRIGHT, THE DRAGON OF FORTUNE

We left the Magicarium and continued trekking toward the tallest tower, where the Dragon of Fortune was waiting for us. By then I was huffing and puffing like a passenger train on the New Mouse City Express! Plus, the golden hatbox and Wolfy's luggage weighed a ton. How much could one little wizard pack? "The Magicarium is . . . **puff** . . . really . . . **puff** . . . extraordinary! It almost seemed like . . . **puff** . . . it was alive," I told Wolfy.

Finally, we reached a SMALL DOOR . . . entered a narrow stairway . . .

and climbed . . . and climbed . . . and climbed . . . and climbed . . . and climbed . . . and climbed . . . and climbed

. . . and the golden hatbox
   was
      heavy . . .
         and heavier . . .
         and heavier . . .
until finally we reached the
top of the highest tower and
saw a dragon. He was
SPARKLING

with the light of
the first stars of the
evening. And he was
ENORMOUSE!

   It was really him . . .

LIGHTBRIGHT,
THE
DRAGON OF FORTUNE

Puff!
Pant!

LIGHTBRIGHT,
THE
DRAGON OF FORTUNE

ROAR!!!

Besides the enormouse dragon, I was hoping a few of the wizards might have gathered at the top of the tower to say good-bye. Maybe with a **CAKE** or BALLOONS or a *three piece band* or . . . Well, okay, I didn't really expect all of that, but a wave good-bye would have been nice. After all, who knew if we would even make it back alive!

But when I mentioned it to Wolfy, she just snorted, "No one dares to climb up here. LIGHTBRIGHT isn't exactly what you would call a friendly dragon."

Before I could say another word a huge voice thundered,

ROOOaaRRR!

I was so scared I nearly jumped out of my fur!

The dragon roared again and said, "I know who she is — she's Wolfy, Mel's niece. And that scrap METAL is my old friend, Ranger, the Ghost Guardian. But I've never seen you before, mouse. Give me one good reason why I shouldn't incinerate you!"

Moldy mozzarella! If only I could blink my eyes and wake up in my cozy mouse home! I tried blinking but nothing happened. Rats! So instead, I stammered, "I need a ride to Dark Castle so I can find the Winged Ring and save Blossom . . ."

He interrupted me again. "Tell me something I don't know. Everyone in the Kingdom of Fantasy is talking about it. They also say that you're the fool who lost the ring in the first place!"

Wolfy approached the dragon, staring

him right in the eyes. I must say, the dragon's eyes were pretty spectacular. They were as clear as water and as bright as the stars. *

"Dear **LIGHTBRIGHT**," she said calmly. "My uncle gave me permission to ask you for a ride. And well, we're sort of in a rush."

At that moment, the pendant of the secret alliance that I had around my neck lit up in the moonlight. The dragon saw it and smiled for the first time.

Dear Lightbright . . .

"He is wearing the **pendant** of the secret alliance. If Blossom gave it to him, that means that she trusts him, so I will, too," he said, lowering his head. "Now climb aboard and I'll take you to **Dark Castle** before the sun comes up!"

Wolfy and Ranger climbed on the dragon's back, and I followed with all the bags. Then the dragon leaped into the air.

WHOOSH!

And he began to flap his powerful wings . . .

It was then that we heard a little voice yell out, "Wait! I'm coming, too!"

We turned to the right, but we didn't see anyone!

HOW STRANGE!

We turned to the left but still no one!

HOW VERY STRANGE!

We looked behind us but again, nothing!

HOW VERY, VERY STRANGE!

Then finally we looked up and saw . . . the

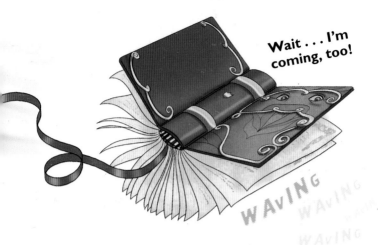

Wait . . . I'm coming, too!

WAvING WAVING WAVING

Magicarium, FLYING toward us like a butterfly, *WAVING* his pages like they were wings! He landed on the dragon's back, and Wolfy grabbed his spine. Lift off!

Oooh! Incredible!

Look, the Magicarium!

As we rose into the sky I turned back to see all the wizards of the great council and all the students from the school of magic waving. I spotted Beartina, Owlivia, Roxy, and even the Von Wild brothers.

They had all come to say good-bye after all!

Then the sky lit up with a magical wish . . .

Have a good trip, friends!

THE KINGDOM OF WITCHES

Where it is told of how Foolish One reached Wither's palace, the terrifying Dark Castle . . .

I DID IT AGAIN!

he Dragon of Fortune waved his powerful wings, *and flew...*

and flew and flew and flew...and flew and flew...and flew...and flew...and flew...and flew...and flew...and flew...and flew...and flew...and flew...and flew...and flew...and flew...and flew...and flew...

"Well, I have to say, I did it again! If it weren't for MIE, we would have never even made it this far. Thanks to me we'll reach Dark Castle before DAWN!"

The Magicarium rustled his pages.

Flip Flip Flip Flip Flip Flip Flip Flip

"Far be it from me to brag, but if it weren't for me, we'd have no secret spells to battle the witch," he insisted.

Creak. Creak. Creak. The Ghost Guardian leaned forward. "Don't kid yourself. If it weren't for me, we might as well turn around right now. I'm the only one who knows how to fight!" he bragged.

Lightbright let out a FLAME-filled snort. "NEWSFLASH! Who is taking you to Dark Castle in one night? If it weren't for me, this whole journey would be a bust!" he sniffed.

As everyone argued we started speeding through the sky so fast I saw stars!

I didn't know if I could take any more SQUABBLING, so I reminded my new friends that we would be much better off if we worked together. "There's no 'I' in team!" I added, quoting my great-uncle Longwhiskers.

From that moment on the quarreling stopped and we flew in ρ℮αc℮ until I realized something was wrong . . .

A really strong wind was pushing against us, and it was cold and stinky. Rancid rat hairs! *It was the evil northern wind!*

It was harder and harder for the dragon to move forward. He was growing more and more

TIRED . . . AND TIRED . . .
TIRED . . . AND TIRED . . .

The flaps of his wings became weaker and weaker and weaker and our trip seemed to go more and more slowly . . . slowly . . . slowly . . . slowly . . . slowly . . . slowly . . .

owly . . . slowly . . . slowly . . . slowly . . . slowly . . . slowly . . .

wly . . . slowly . . . slowly . . . slowly . . . slowly . . . slowly . . .

Mel's words came to mind: *"Remember to get there before the sun rises, because the* starry dragon *will vanish at the first rays of sun!"*

Oh no. A chill ran down my fur. The sky was BRIGHTENING all around us. There wasn't much time left. The sun struggled to peek out over the horizon. We had to get LIGHTBRIGHT to fly faster, but how?

"Maybe if I sing the secret dragon song," mumbled LIGHTBRIGHT. "That always gets me going." He tipped his head back and sang,

The dragon sped up, but still it wasn't enough.

I sing with a voice that's loud,
So I fly fast and proud,
I'm fierce and strong and tough,
And if that's not enough,
Then hear my fiery roar,
And you will see me soar!

As the sun's rays *pierced* the sky, the dragon VANISHED in a flash! And we fell down.

Holey cheese balls, I thought that I would be splattered like a mouse omelet!

Instead I fell on a soft pile of leaves in a swamp.
"I'm **SAFE**! I didn't even get one
scratch . . ." I started to say when Ranger fell on
my head . . .

Bonk!

Then Wolfy . . .

BAANG!

Then the Magicarium . . .

And finally the bags and the (extremely heavy)
solid-gold hatbox . . .

KABOOOM!

At which point I *fainted!*

SPOILED CHEESE AND ROTTEN EGGS!

hen I opened my eyes I almost fainted again from the smell.

The wind was *blowing* the incredible, indescribable, unmistakable stench of

witch!

It smelled like withered flowers, rotten mold, **stinky diapers**, sour milk, spoiled cheese, and rotten eggs!

We had arrived in the Kingdom of Witches! Far off in the swamp I saw the shadow of two castles. One was Cackle's castle. I recognized it immediately, because I had already been there on one of my previous adventures.

The other **castle** was the one I had seen in the ball of marvels. It was Dark Castle, the new **BEWITCHED** castle that Wither had built in one night!

That was where we needed to go . . .

BUT WOULD WE BE ABLE TO RETURN WITHIN ONE MOON CYCLE?

KINGDOM OF WITCHES

1. Dark Castle
2. Pale Ghost Peak
3. Wicked Witch Woods
4. Black Swamp
5. Lake of Tears
6. River of Regret
7. Bare Bones Desert
8. Restless Ghost Cemetery
9. Buzz Buzz Swamp
10. Moldy Mountain
11. Nightmare Forest
12. Giant Scorpions
13. Fortress of Fear

Do We Have to Go In?

s we trudged toward the Dark Castle my fur got **PLASTERED** with mud, and gnats flew in my ears. If only I could take a hot, *cheesy* bubble bath!

Meanwhile, the vultures stared at us with evil eyes . . .

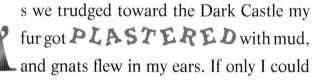

How scary! How terrifying! How fur-raising!

"All right everyone, here's the plan," Wolfy announced as we walked. "We'll knock on the castle door and I'll say that I am **WITCH SLYELLA** of the Seven Scams. I come from the faraway Dukedom of Slyville and I'm here to attend the Great Witch Council. I've brought with me GRUMBLEDUMPY, my pet OGRE (the Prince); and my bodyguard (Ranger, the Ghost Guardian). Then I will hold up the solid-GOLD hatbox with the spy hat inside and explain that I have brought a very special gift for Wither."

Just as Wolfy finished speaking, we looked up and saw a menacing castle before us. It was Dark Castle!

How scary! How fur-raising! How terrifying!

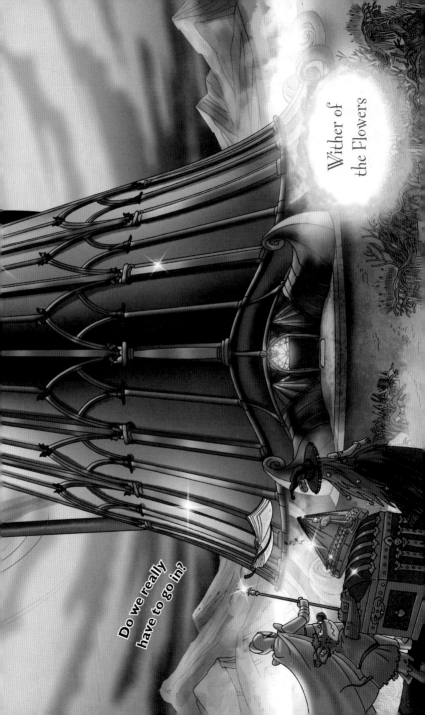

"DO WE REALLY HAVE TO GO IN?
DO WE REALLY HAVE TO GO IN?
DO WE REALLY HAVE TO GO IN?"

I whined.

"Get a grip!" she commanded. "We're going in whether you like it or not. And remember you need to act like a real ogre. Lots of **burping**, **grumbling**, and **nonstop farting**!

Are you sure we have to do this?

Let's do it!

Let's go!

I'm ready!

TOOT! TOOT! TOOT! TOOT! TOOT! POFFF! TOOT! TOOT!

"Plus, I can't be nice to you in there," she warned. "Witches are mean to their ogres."

"Fine," I said with a sigh. Who says *Geronimo Stilton* is not a team player?!

The Magicarium closed his eyes and clamped his pages shut so you couldn't tell that he was a **living book**.

Then Wolfy took a long, deep breath and said *"Okay, let's go!"*

Knock! Knock!

Fearfully, we approached the castle. Squeak, what a terrible **witch stench**! Then I knocked on the door.

But no one opened.

I tried again.

KNOCK! KNOCK!

But there was only silence.

I gathered my courage and tried one more time.

KNOCK! KNOCK!

This time a deep voice yelled, "Hey, do you have **WOOD** for brains? Don't you know you need to knock **three times** on a bewitched castle door?"

I jumped back. "Who said that?!"

"Who do you think is talking, oak-tree brain? I am, **the door**, obviously!"

Two big evil eyes and an enormouse mouth appeared on the door.

Then it thundered, "Are you coming in or not? I have other things to do with my time!"

The D°°RMAT added, "But first wipe your feet, ogre!"

We entered and the door closed suddenly. Badabang!

A marble sculpture was pointing to a stairway. "Hurry up!" the sculpture said. "Go that way, to the Witch's Stairway!"

The carpet I was walking on **yelled**, "Come on, what are you waiting for?"

Along the walls there were PORTRAITS of famous witches.

I tried not to shiver when I spotted the

biggest portrait of all. It was of her! You know, **WITHER**!

A **VULTURE** demanded Wolfy's documents and she showed him her (fake!) witch `ID card`. "I'm here for the Great Witch Council. This is Grumbledumpy, my **OGRE**; and my bodyguard.

WITCH ID CARD

NAME: Slyella of the Seven Scams
RESIDENCE: Dukedom of Slyville
DATE OF BIRTH: the third full moon of the year of the Fire Dragon
PROFESSION: witchery
SPECIALIZATION: specializes in spells of craftiness
DISTINGUISHING TRAITS: wart on her nose

WELCOME TO DARK CASTLE!

THE MOST LUXURIOUSLY BEWITCHED CASTLE IN ALL OF THE KINGDOM OF FANTASY

Breakfast is served at moonrise. Be on time: Chef Trollee is very touchy! If you arrive late, you will end up as food for her vampire bats!

The Great Witch Council will be held at midnight on the dot. You must choose Wither or Cackle to be your Dark Queen!

OH, THIS OLD THING?

With a glance, the vulture checked Wolfy over. He looked at her hat and the binding of the Magicarium and the silver armor of the Ghost Guardian. But he was especially interested in the **golden hatbox**.

"Great goose feathers! What have we here?"

Wolfy replied, "Oh, this old thing? It's just a tiny little **GIFT** for Wither."

She sniffed and added, "It contains a witch's

How magnificent!

hat identical to my own woven with SILK THREAD, adorned with a giant **ruby**, and decorated with an exquisite BLACK PEARL."

Then she offered gold coins to the vulture. "Can you send this to Wither on my behalf?" she added.

The vulture pocketed the money, squawking, "Oh, of course, dear Lady Slyella. I will give it to Wither, our Dark Lady. And I hope you will be happy in our very best room in the castle, Bewitched Room Number Thirteen, in the Hat's tower, with a panoramic view of Buzz Buzz Swamp!"

Wolfy gave the vulture another handful of coins and he bowed. "Thank you, Lady Slyella. I am at your service. My name is **Dismal**, but you can call me Dissy."

Meanwhile, a really **LONG** line of witches had formed and they had begun to complain.

"Come on!"

"What's taking so long?"

"It's nearly nightfall!"

Dismal cawed, "**Gulls and skulls**, you must excuse me, Lady Slyella, I must check in the other guests. Remember the Great Witch Council begins at **MIDNIGHT**!"

Come on! What's taking so long? It's nearly nightfall!

Dismal gave Slyella the map of the castle and the key to our room.

"Grumbledumpy, bring my trunk to room number **thirteen**!" she ordered, stomping her foot.

I lifted the **HEAVY** trunk over my head. **OUCH!**

Grumbledumpy, hurry up!

Ouch!

WITHER'S CASTLE

1. Slyella's room
2. Queen Wither's apartments
3. Northern wind factory
4. Guest rooms
5. Library
6. The Thousand Eyes Cell
7. The Great Witch Council room
8. Witch Tailor
9. Witch School
10. Stinky Shoe Store
11. Wicked Outfitters
12. Dark, Dank Dining Hall
13. Witch Gym
14. Ugly Salon
15. Armory
16. Entrance
17. Broom parking lot

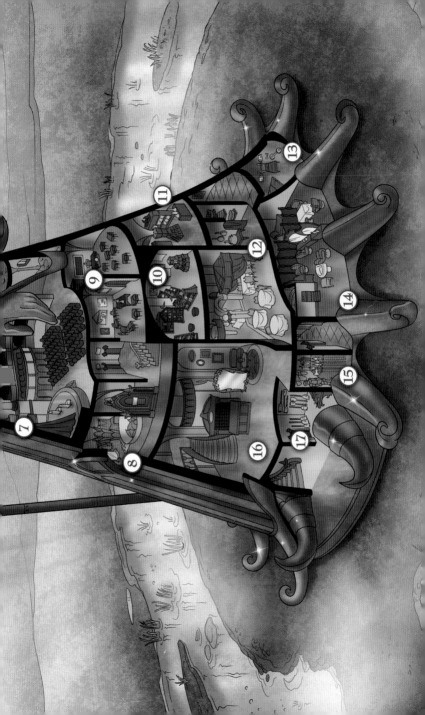

PEE-YOO!

We followed the map as we headed through the bewitched castle. It was full of **trapdoors** and bewitched objects. There were carpets that tripped you, **prankster** mirrors that changed your appearance, and tail-pinching doors that (what else!) pinched your tail! The pictures on the walls stuck out their tongues and the statues bopped you on the head!

The suits of armor standing in the hallways POKED me. Then they tried to pick a fight with

There were tripping carpets ...

Oops!

... prankster mirrors ...

the Ghost Guardian. What a scary sight!

Dark Castle was equipped with everything that a witch could need. There was a special SALON, a wicked clothing and accessories store, and a **dark, dank dining hall**. We even passed a witch shoe store where witches were trying on the latest footwear.

Pee-yoo! The STENCH was awful!

... tail-pinching doors ...

... rude pictures, and ...

... poking armor!

Wicked Outfitters

Answer on page 574

Where is the Warty Toad?

If you need a brand-new broom, a magic wand, or a new witch hat, you'll find it here at Wicked Outfitters. We even have ingredients for magic potions from *A* for Aggressive Aardvarks to *Z* for Zebra Zombies!

Answer on page 574

How many lice do you see in the salon?

In this salon you will become more horrendous than ever, thanks to our team of lice who specialize in aesthetic treatments! Pimpleton the louse will make enormouse warts grow on your face. Dentalton will give you the perfect toothless witch's sneer. Clipperton will put knots in your hair, and Facialton will turn your skin a sickly yellow.

WITCH TAILOR

How many vultures are at the tailor's?

Answer on page 575

Calvin Stickpin, the witchiest fashion designer in the kingdom, will advise you on the best dress for every occasion! Veils of giant spiders, bat wings, roach and green-beetle rhinestones, and the scales of the Giant Salivating Centipede will adorn your most horrific garments.

STINKY SHOE STORE
WITCH SHOES FOR
ALL OCCASIONS

Answer on page 575

Find the other shoe that matches this one!

Any self-respecting witch needs shoes worthy of her stinky feet! We have evening wear, swamp boots, flying shoes (that latch to your broom and never fall off!), no-slip witch slippers, and more!

Dark, Dank DINING HALL

How many trolls can you count in the dining hall?

Attention: Dark dress required — no exceptions!
Please park brooms in the designated parking
lot. All magic assistants must wait outside where
they will be provided with refreshments including
rotten algae stew and snake-pee pasta.

Answer on page 575

GROSSELDA GRIMWITCH

*You will find the Fantasian alphabet on page 571.

e had almost reached our room when we met a cat with black **fur** wearing a magician's long starry cloak. It was . . .

THE MENACE, CHATTERING CAT!

So this was Wither's witch assistant!

I recognized him from the Ball of Marvels.

He was sharpening his claws with a nail file and guarding a door that had Fantasian writing on it.*

He stared at us suspiciously and said, "Meow! I am Menace, the Chattering Cat! And who, **MEOW**, are you?"

I tried to stay calm. Seeing a cat was bad

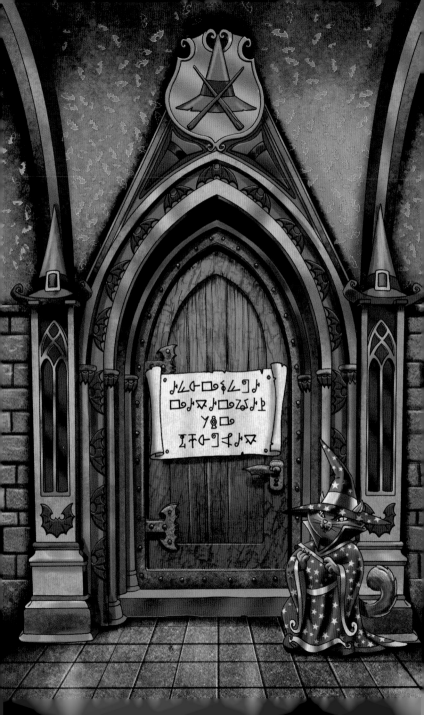

Magic hat

White hair

Keys to
the witch
school

Menace, the Chattering Cat!

He is the guardian of the witch school and has a very desired position. He is Wither's personal witch assistant! He has dark, shiny black fur and one white hair on the tip of his tail. According to witch tradition, the best witch assistants are black cats with one single piece of white hair.

His passion is telling magic jokes (though they are *purr*fectly awful!). His responsibilities include: polishing Wither's magic wand every day with wasp poison, ironing her cloak, shopping for magic potions, guarding the witch school, and chasing rats (rat soup is one of the witches' favorite dishes).

But above all his most important and secret duty is eavesdropping to find out the juiciest gossip to tell Wither!

enough, but a cat who worked for a **wicked witch** was enough to make me **PASS OUT** on the spot! "I'm, um, Grumbledumpy, the ogre and, uh, this is my owner, the wizard, I mean, the witch Slyella," I mumbled.

Menace sniffed. "Meow! You don't smell like an ogre," he said. "You smell like a, meow, mouse! And you don't act like an ogre. You act like a mouse!"

Just then I remembered what the wizard had told me about acting like an ogre. I let out a loud . . . **burp**! And an even louder . . . toot!

"Slyella likes mice. That's why I smell like them," I lied.

I have no idea if the cat bought my fib because suddenly we heard Wither's cackle. "MEEEENAAACCEEE! I need you! Hurry up, you sack of fleas!"

He ran away, huffing, "**MEOW!** Coming, my

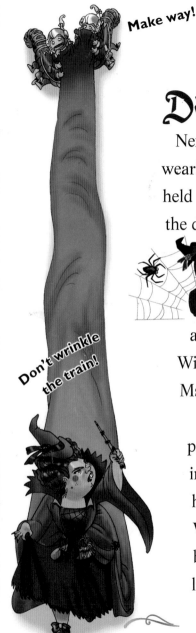

Make way!

Don't wrinkle the train!

Dark Queen!"

Next, a witch walked by wearing a long train that was held by two bugs. "Make way for the director of the witch school, **GROSSELDA GRIMWITCH**, aka Teacher of All Things Witchy, aka Lady of Drool, aka Ms. Gross, coming through!"

As soon as the procession passed by, Wolfy whispered in my ear: "Those fools are headed for a miserable life. Witches have no friends because they are mean, nasty liars. Yep, being a WITCH

IS NOT PRETTY!

IT'S NOT FUN!

AND IT'S SUPER GROSS

AND STINKY!

"The worst part about being a witch is that they can only use magic to do bad things," Wolfy added. "What **FUN** is that?"

Curious, I peeked inside the classroom. There were a lot of little witches telling bad **witch jokes** . . .

BAD WITCH JOKES

WHY ARE SOME EELS ELECTRIC?
BECAUSE THERE'S A CURRENT IN THE WATER!

WHY COULDN'T THE SALAD SLEEP?
BECAUSE IT TOSSED!

WHY WERE THE CURTAINS ARTISTIC?
BECAUSE THEY WERE DRAWN!

Hee, hee, hee!

Ha, ha, ha!

Ho, ho, ho!

WHY IS THE CALENDAR ALWAYS SAD?
BECAUSE ITS DAYS ARE NUMBERED!

HOW DO OCEANS SAY HI?  THEY WAVE!

WHY DOESN'T THE TURKEY GAMBLE? IT'S AFRAID OF GETTING ITS FEATHERS RIPPED OFF!

WHY IS THE MORNING AIR SO COLD? BECAUSE IT STAYS OUT ALL NIGHT LONG!

WHY IS A HEADACHE SO GOOD IN SCHOOL? BECAUSE IT ALWAYS PASSES!

DARK WITCH SCHOOL

Answer on page 576

How many witches can you count in the school?

The exclusive witch school founded by Wither of the Flowers only gives a diploma to those who have proven themselves truly ugly, truly evil, and truly stinky! In addition to your diploma, you receive a witch hat, magic wand, broom, and witch's assistant!

THE RULES OF THE
DARK WITCH SCHOOL

❖ 1 ❖ All students must wear the uniform: a black cape that goes down to your feet with bat-wing-shaped sleeves and the emblem of the witch school with its motto: "Badder is better!"

❖ 2 ❖ All students must respect the school hours. Classes begin at midnight and end at dawn.

❖ 3 ❖ All students must never brush their hair, take a bath, brush their teeth, cut their nails, or change their socks for at least a year, and they must smell like a trash can in summertime! Basically, the stinkier they are, the better!

❖ 4 ❖ All students must obey the director, Grosselda Grimwitch, who can expel anyone if they are caught doing something nice!

❖ 5 ❖ All students must take care of their helpers including feeding them, walking them, and picking up their droppings. Otherwise they will be fined.

GrosSelda Grimwitch

List of students to fail

Keys to all the rooms

Magic wand

Silk spider dress

Witch helpers

Superlong train

Dragon-skin shoes

Grosselda is the stinkiest, most untrustworthy traitor in the Kingdom of Fantasy. She was Cackle's advisor until she betrayed her when Wither became the most powerful witch. In exchange, Wither has named her the director of the Dark Witch School.

Ms. Gross has a weak spot for shoes. She has hundreds of them, and they are all stinky!

Her helpers are two giant bugs, Bugeroo and Bugadoo, who hold her long train and shine her shoes three times a day!

The Hat Tower

fter we left the classroom, we began climbing the steep steps leading to the

Hat Tower.

"Are we there yet? I need to **OIL** my joints," the Ghost Guardian huffed.

"This place is so humid. I better not get **mold** on my pages," the *Magicarium* whined.

If you ask me, I should have been the one **COMPLAINING**. I was carrying Wolfy's **heavy** luggage and the book. If only books had legs!

Holey cheese balls, I was exhausted!

When we passed a **CLOCK** on the wall I shivered.

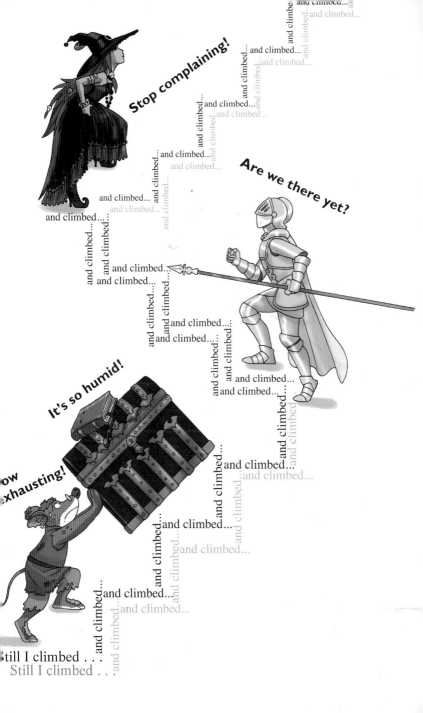

TIME WAS FLYING! WOULD WE MAKE IT BACK BY ONE MOON CYCLE?

Finally, we reached the top of the stairs and there was our room, room number **13**! Could we be more unlucky?!

When I opened the door, I gasped. It was a dark, dank, stinky mess. There were thorns on the blankets, cobwebs in every corner, and a table full of stinky food in the middle of the room. What a nightmare!

The **gloomy** room had a view of the

Quickly, I helped Wolfy get ready for the Great Witch Council. She teased her hair and sprayed

herself with STINKY perfume. She dusted her face with dead-roach powder and sprinkled glitter on her broom. At last she was ready.

"Let's go!" she said bravely. "It's almost midnight."

Answer on page 576

DONG! DONG! DONG!

At that moment, a bell began to ring: DONG, DONG, DONG, DONG, DONG, DONG, DONG, DONG, DONG, DONG, DONG, DONG...

Twelve gongs, it was **MIDNIGHT**!

We quickly went down the stairs and reached the entrance to the Great Witch Council. But **Dismal** blocked our entrance. "Invitation, please!" he demanded.

Wolfy turned to me. "Grumbledumpy, show Mr. Dismal the *invitation*!" she commanded.

I turned pale because (obviously!) we didn't have an invitation. I muttered, "Well . . . um . . . er . . ."

She gave me a **kick** in the tail. "You left it at home, didn't you, ogre?!" she shrieked.

Then she turned to the vulture, "Ah, Mr. Dismal,

you can't find good help anymore. Am I right or am I right?"

She sighed dramatically. "Alas, I've come from so very far away. Anyway, can you CUT me a break here, Mr. Dismal? Or should I call you D?"

Dismal extended his mangy wing and Wolfy gave him a sack of GOLD MONEY.

The vulture bowed low. "Young Lady Slyella, please go ahead, there are three seats in the orchestra section for you!"

Ooouuch!

It's all your fault!

Hmm...

Then he stepped aside and we entered

the Great Witch Council Room.

Inside the room the witches were behaving like, well, witches. They were screaming and yelling and throwing around **rotten** tomatoes and eggs.

I spotted Grosselda and then Menace. As soon as I entered the room the cat began to sniff around suspiciously. **SNIFF! SNIFF! SNIFF!**

Squeak, how scary!

Wolfy quickly sat down because the two **ENEMIES** Cackle and Wither were already taking their seats. Wither was wearing the **Spy Hat**, which sparkled under the lights. Right then the crowd became SILENT.

I noticed Cackle wore a worried expression instead of her usual evil one. How odd. Was her face on a SCOWLING strike?

At that exact moment a black crow with a copper beak burst through a window, sending broken glass flying everywhere. **"Caaaaww! Caaaaww!"** He settled

Sniff sniff sniff...

caw! caw! caw!

on the ground next to Wither. Then he began to spin around and around so fast, just watching him made my eyes water. Too bad ogres don't carry tissues!

When the bird finally stopped **spinning**, he had transformed into a dark-haired prince. It was **Crowbar the Cruel**, the Prince of Darkness!

Answer on page 576

Crowbar, or should I say the prince, whispered something in Wither's ear. Wither giggled. Then he said, "You look beautiful. Love the dress." And Wither replied, "Oh, this old thing, I just pulled it out of the **dirty laundry**."

The prince beamed. "Nice! Clean laundry is so disgusting." Wither nodded, staring **dreamily** into the prince's eyes.

For a minute the whole room just watched the two, transfixed. Did they realize they were **gabbing** in the middle of a meeting of the

GREAT WITCH COUNCIL?

Eventually, Cackle interrupted. "I hate to break up this party, you two, but we are here to decide who will be the next queen. It's up to the **WITCH POPULATION**!"

Then Cackle turned to all the witches. "**Vote**

for me and we will conquer the entire Kingdom of Fantasy!" she shrieked.

Wither **laughed** scornfully. "The Kingdom of Fantasy is just the tip of the iceberg for me. If you vote for me, we will have power over the whole **universe**!"

Then she lifted her hand up to reveal a sparkling ring. "I've got it! I've got the

winged ring!"

Wither laughed shrilly.

"The ring lets me travel between worlds! It has enormous power! A vote for me will mean power over everything!"

Then Menace, Wither's assistant, stood up. "If you want Cackle, put a WHITE stone in the

This better count!

Meow!

Hurry up!

Get it done

ballot bowl. If you want Wither, put a **black** stone in."

When it was time to count the **STONES**, everyone sat on the edge of their seats.

Wither paced back and forth. Cackle chewed her nails.

But as soon as Menace emptied the ballot bowl it was clear who the winner was. All the stones were **black**!

"I won!" Wither yelled, breaking out her dance moves. She did the **Bad Broom** (spinning like a cyclone) and the **WICKED WITCH WALK** (moonwalking while cackling).

Then she ripped the wand from Cackle's grip. "Leave at once!" she shouted. "There's a new Queen in town!"

Cackle stormed off screaming, "I'll be back!" over her shoulder.

And all the witches sang,

"Life is strange, go figure,
long live great Queen Wither!
A friend of Cackle's she seemed to be,
but now she is her enemy!
She's got the ring and all its power
and Cackle has to leave the tower!"

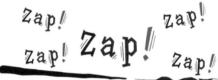

ZAP!

o celebrate Wither's victory the witches let out bolts of lightning with their magic wands.

zap! zap! **Zap!** zap! zap! zap!

A flame singed my whisker.

Without thinking I yelled at the top of my lungs,

"Squeeeeak!"

Silence fell over the room and all the witches turned toward me.

Menace stalked over to me, licking his whiskers. "Meow! Meow! Meow! I knew it! You squeak like a **mouse**, you stink like a **mouse**, you even have ears like a **mouse**! You're no ogre . . . **you are a mouse**!"

Wither turned and glared at me closely. "**Sour spider spit!** I recognize you! You're the prince, no, I mean, you're the Foolish One, my goody-two-shoes sister, Blossom's, little friend! You're the **furbrain** who let me steal the ring!" she cackled.

Suddenly, Wither squinted at Wolfy. She **muttered**, "Hey, you, with the hat like mine!

You remind me of someone . . . but who?"

Then she shouted, "I **RECOGNIZE** you, you're Wolfy! You are the niece of my sister's greatest friend, and my **worst** enemy,

Ha, ha! What luck! You're my hostage now!"

Wither grabbed my **bag** and rummaged through it until she found the *Magicarium*. "Well, looky looky, this is Mel the Magnificent's precious book of spells! It really is my lucky day! I should buy a lottery ticket!"

Then she threw the bag out the **window** without realizing that OPEN-UP, the enchanted key, was still inside.

She waved her wand at the magic book, shrieking, "The power of FIRE is great and

It's my lucky day! The Magicarium!

just, I'll turn this book into ASH DUST!"

The flames crackled, surrounding the book. I closed my eyes — it was too sad to watch the 𝓜𝖆𝖌𝖎𝖈𝖆𝖗𝖎𝖚𝖒 burn.

But when I opened them, my jaw hit the floor. The flames hadn't

a single page!

"Oooh, that Magicarium is truly magic!"

all the witches exclaimed.

ZAP!

Wither was furious. She grabbed the book from the fire, picked up a pair of razor-sharp scissors, and cried,

"MAGIC BLADES, hold on steady, make this book into confetti!"

Immediately, the silver scissors began to **CUT**. Well . . . they tried to cut, but it was impossible to cut the pages of that magic **book**!

Annoyed, Wither threw the scissors to the ground and they

clinked and clanked as they bounced!

CLANK! CLANK! CLANK!

The witches were more and more impressed, and Wither was more and more ANNOYED.

HMMMM. HMMMM. HMMMM,

she THOUGHT and THOUGHT and THOUGHT.

Then the witch Grosselda whispered something in Wither's ear. The new Dark Queen lit up. "Yes, yes. You've got something there. What irritates a book? Being BURNED, being CUT or . . . getting WET! And I've got the perfect muddy, smelly water a book would hate!" She snickered.

Without another word she opened the window and threw the book out, right into the stinky moat surrounding the castle!

I watched in horror as the book sank into the water in a cloud of bubbles.

Tears came to my eyes.

The poor Magicarium!

Wither said, snickering, "As for you, I will use you as *hostages* to get everything I want from good old Mel!"

It was already dawn when seven Dark Knights appeared. They were led by their grim leader, **Bleak** of the seven Dark Knights. "You will follow me to the most secure prison in the kingdom, the **THOUSAND EYES CELL**!" he announced.

He snatched Wolfy's wand and snapped it in two. Snap! "Let's go!" he ordered.

But Wither held up her hand. "Not so fast, little wizard!" she screeched at Wolfy. "Do you really think I was born last century? I know you wizards carry more than one wand around!"

She LIFTED Wolfy's sleeve and pulled out a second, SMALLER wand.

THE WITCHES CHEERED!

Our queen
is extraordinary,
nasty, vile, and super scary!
She's pure evil at its best
from the east and
to the west!

THE THOUSAND
EYES CELL

*You can find the Fantasian alphabet on page 571.

The seven Dark Knights, led by Bleak and Menace the cat, dragged us to a small black door that was locked by **seven bronze locks**.

There was a sign written in Fantasian.*

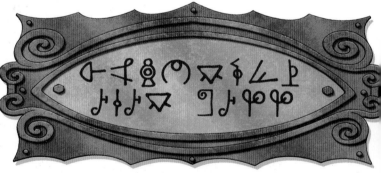

The Dark Knights pushed us through the door, and up a dark, narrow stairway . . .

As we climbed up that nightmarish stairway, the knights poked us with their spears. **Youch!**

Right then Menace let out a loud meow! "Who poked me in the tail?" he whined, staring at us suspiciously.

How strange!

Why would the knights be attacking the cat? Then I heard Wolfy chuckling to herself. Something told me she still had some magic up her sleeve even if she had lost her wand!

Finally, we reached a cell as **DARK** as night. The knights shoved us inside and bolted the door.

SQUEAK! I'M AFRAID OF THE DARK!

The Thousand Eyes Cell
To imprison her victims, Wither created this bewitched prison that no one can escape from. (Well, actually there is a way to escape, but only Wither and Grosselda know the secret. Shhh!)

Suddenly, I noticed something strange. There were many tiny blinking lights throughout the cell. Then it hit me. These weren't lights, they were **HUNDREDS AND HUNDREDS OF EYES**! There were eyes on the wall, eyes on the ceiling, and even eyes on the floor!

Now I knew why this place was called the Thousand Eyes Cell. We were being watched by **A THOUSAND EYES**!

HOW WOULD WE EVER ESCAPE? HOW WOULD WE MAKE IT BACK WITHIN ONE MOON CYCLE?!

I was about to begin sobbing like a mouselet when we heard footsteps.

"Shhh . . . Someone is coming," Wolfy whispered.

A minute later the door opened a crack and a whiskered snout poked through the small opening. Then a scratchy feline voice began to meow a lullabye . . .

Who's that?!

Go to sleep!

"Time to sleep so shut your eyes.
Your lids feel heavy, oversized.
You are tired, you need sleep.
So close your eyes, don't make a peep!"

One by one the thousand eyes began to close.
And the sound of snoring filled the room.

SNORE!

SNOOORE!

SNOOOOORE!

A minute later, Menace the cat meowed, "Pssst, meow, I need to talk to you, wizard lady!"

How odd. What could the cat want from a jailbird? Or should I say, jailwizard?!

"Lady Wolfy, I know you stole my only WHITE HAIR and I want it back!" the cat hissed. "Without that **magic** hair I have no **magic** powers. I'm just a kitty without a clue! A **PURRFECTLY** plain old feline! Meow, how embarrassing!"

Wolfy snickered. "I've got good news and bad news for you," she said. Then she lowered her voice. "The good news is that I do have your white hair. The bad news is that to get it back you must help us **escape from this creepy eyeball prison**!"

At this the cat began meowing up a storm. He sounded like he just lost the winning ticket to a lifetime supply of **tuna ROLLS**. "Meow, I want my hair! I want my magic! I want my mommy!" he wailed.

Wolfy held firm. "No escape, no hair!" she insisted.

Lucky for us the cat agreed. I couldn't wait to get out of there. Even though the thousand eyes were shut, all of that **snoring** was enough to send me straight to the **madmouse center**!

"Just don't tell the boss I helped you escape," the cat pleaded. "If Wither finds out, she'll **incinerate** me!"

Hmmm . . .

I want my hair!

GET OUT!

enace pushed us down the stone steps of a spiral staircase. Luckily it was only **MIDDAY** and all the witches were sleeping. It didn't take us long to reach the exit.

At the exit, Wolfy gave Menace his magical

Get out!

We're going! We're going!

white hair. He shoved it in the

GOLD MEDALLION

he wore around his neck for safekeeping.

Then the cat pushed us out, warning us to never tell how we escaped.

He slammed the door behind us with a thud.

THUD!

I sighed. Don't get me wrong, I was thrilled to get out of the prison, but we still hadn't found the Winged Ring. "If only we could find the **SAFE** that holds the ring," I muttered aloud.

To my surprise, Wolfy was already ten steps ahead of me. "You **UNDERESTIMATE** me, Prince." She laughed. "Thanks to the

two spy hats

I already know where the safe is!"

It turned out the safe was in Wither's **secret laboratory**, which was the safest room in the castle. I wondered what made it safe. Was it guarded by a **two-headed monster**? Or a FIRE-BREATHING DRAGON?

Tell us!

I know where the ring is!

Where?

"But, Wolfy, how will we find this room?" I asked.

"No problem," the young wizard replied. "We just need to get the 𝓜𝓪𝓰𝓲𝓬𝓪𝓻𝓲𝓾𝓶 back. He wasn't destroyed when he fell in the moat. He's magical and therefore he is **INDESTRUCTIBLE**. He can find the *secret laboratory*. There's only one little problem.

You will have to JUMP in the moat to get him, Prince."

I blinked. "M-M-M-ME?" I stammered.

"Yes, you! Ranger can't go in the water because his joints will RUST. It's up to you, Prince," Wolfy insisted. Then she added, "Just remember to watch out for the swamp crocodiles and the fanged fish and the poisonous ticklish serpents."

BITTER CHEDDAR BISCUITS!

Instantly my whiskers began whirling with fear. In fact, they started **WHIRLING** so fast they lifted me off the ground and I flew far, far away never to be seen again! Okay, okay, that didn't really happen but you get the picture. I was SCARED out of my fur!

"Don't worry, Knight! As my uncle Mel says, there's a SOLUTION to every problem,"

Wolfy assured me. Then she gave me three tips: 1. Bop the crocodiles on the nose (they had sensitive noses!); 2. Feed the fish COOKIES (so they wouldn't be hungry); and 3. Tickle the serpents (they were super-ticklish!).

Down at the moat we saw lots of tiny bubbles coming up, as if something was **BREATHING** down there . . .

Was it the Magicarium?

If it was the book, why didn't he just swim up? Unfortunately, there was

Ugh, what a stench! Yuck!

only one way to find out. I **plugged** my nose
and jumped in . . .

I swam . . . and swam . . . and I swam . . . and swam . . .
going lower and lower in that dense muddy water.

I saw the snouts of **crocodiles** and,
following Wolfy's advice, bopped their noses. It

A flick here . . .

worked! They backed
away!

Score one for the
mouse!

Next I found myself
facing the SHARP
teeth of the **fanged**

fish! Quickly, I popped the cookies in their mouths. They **SWALLOWED** them up in one bite, then swam away.

A cookie for you . . .

Squeak, all that was left were the dangerous **ticklish serpents**! But as soon as I tickled their tails the serpents slipped away in fits of laughter.

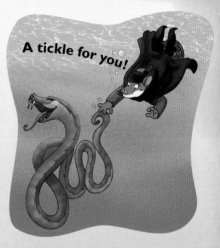

A tickle for you!

I swam **deeper** and, finally, I saw the book. Clasping algae had **BRAIDED** around him and was holding him down. Rats!

I didn't have time to untie the knots so I found a sharp rock and cut the *clasping algae*. *Snip!*

Then I noticed something in the mud, so I grabbed it. It was my bag! I took it, put the $\mathscr{M}$agicarium under my arm, and . . .

I swam . . . and swam . . . and swam . . . toward the surface!

THE RETRIEVAL
OF THE
WINGED RING

Where it is told of how
Foolish One, Wolfy, and
the Ghost Guardian (and
the Magicarium, too!)
attempted to retrieve the
Winged Ring . . .

UP AND DOWN...UP AND DOWN...UP AND DOWN!

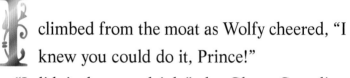 climbed from the moat as Wolfy cheered, "I knew you could do it, Prince!"

"I didn't, but good job," the Ghost Guardian muttered.

Meanwhile, the book flipped his muddy pages.

Mud **splattered** in my direction. Ugh! Now I really resembled a **mud monster**, especially after my swim in that moat! Oh, where was a nice outdoor shower when you needed one?!

"Oops, sorry about that, Foolish One." The book chuckled. "And thanks. You showed real courage. Without you who knows how long I'd be held prisoner by the **clasping algae**! That was one strong plant!"

I turned **red**. "I wasn't really courageous, I was scared," I mumbled.

"Courage is being scared but going on anyway," the book replied. "I know I read that somewhere."

Right then Wolfy interrupted us. It seemed that the spy hat had some news. Wither was sleeping, so it was the perfect time to steal back the Winged Ring.

"If only we had a **magic wand** . . ."

Ghost Guardian lamented.

Things were not looking good. How would we get back into the **Dark Castle** without anyone noticing?

Just when it seemed our adventure had come to an end I noticed Wolfy grinning. Huh? Was her **SPY HAT** telling her jokes? Then she bent down and lifted the hem of her witch's dress. Tied to her ankle was a really TINY wand!

"Every wizard needs THRee MAGiC WANDS!" she announced.

Every wizard needs three magic wands!

Huh?

"The FIRST one is the one they take from you, the SECOND is the one they look for . . . and the THIRD is the one that no one expects to find! And that's the one that can save you!"

Then she pointed the WAND at the Magicarium and said, "Oh magic book, enchanted and bold, show me the secret that's never been told!"

The Magicarium leafed through his pages until he stopped at one page. Suddenly, words appeared on the page . . .

Bigger, stronger, let me fly.
And lift my friends into the sky!

Wolfy repeated the spell over and over until . . .

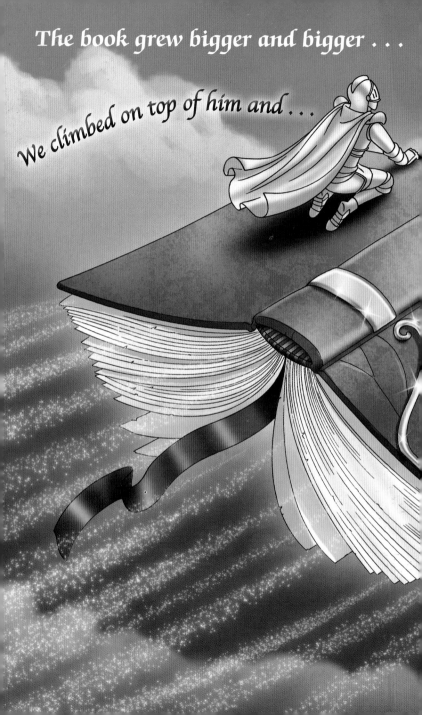

We lifted off into the sky!

We had **ALMOST** reached the top of the tower when the magic broom that made the northern wind began to move

UP AND DOWN...
UP AND DOWN...
UP AND DOWN...
UP AND DOWN...
UP AND DOWN...
UP AND DOWN...
UP AND DOWN...

UP AND DOWN...
UP AND DOWN...
UP AND DOWN...
UP AND DOWN...
UP AND DOWN...
UP AND DOWN...

The strong wind **froze** my fur.

BRRR!

We hung on to the book for dear life, but soon we were all losing our grip.

"**GOOD-BYE**, mouse, it was nice knowing you!" Ghost Guardian yelled.

"**GOOD-BYE**, everyone!" I cried.

Then I closed my eyes, fearing the worst. Would we crash into a rock?

Or slam into the ground? Or smash against the castle wall?

CLICK!

I waited and waited and waited and waited. But nothing happened. Instead, the *Magicarium* somehow managed to fly us safely to a window right outside Wither's **secret laboratory**. The window was covered by thick wooden shutters that were locked. So I pulled out

Open-up, the enchanted key,

and stuck the key in the lock. I turned the key **SLOWLY**, holding my breath. It worked! The shutters opened, so we jumped inside!

Too bad I landed on my tail.

I was about to *cry* out but Wolfy covered my mouth. "**Sssshhh!** We can't let them find us!" she warned.

Answer on page 576

I nodded. I was one step closer to finding the ring. One step closer to leaving **Dark Castle**. One step closer to reuniting with Blossom. One step closer to my cozy home squeak home!

But when Wolfy asked where the safe was located, her hat grumbled, "The other spy hat didn't tell me. And now that **fool** is sleeping!"

We looked everywhere for the **SAFE**.
We looked under tables. We looked
under chairs. We looked in chests and caldrons.

Then suddenly, I **TRIPPED** on a purple
rug in the middle of the room.

I found myself lying on the ground...

SMACK!

Oof!

Right then I noticed that on the ground there was . . . a **KEYHOLE**!

I grabbed Open-up, the enchanted key. I put the key in the keyhole.

I tried and tried and tried and tried and tried to **turn** the key, until all of a sudden it went . . .

A **HATCH** opened and I saw a tiny golden safe locked with . . .

seven locks

Ummm . . .

THE WINGED RING

Thanks to the enchanted key, I opened all seven locks.

And when I opened the safe I found . . . the Winged Ring!

It was so sparkly!

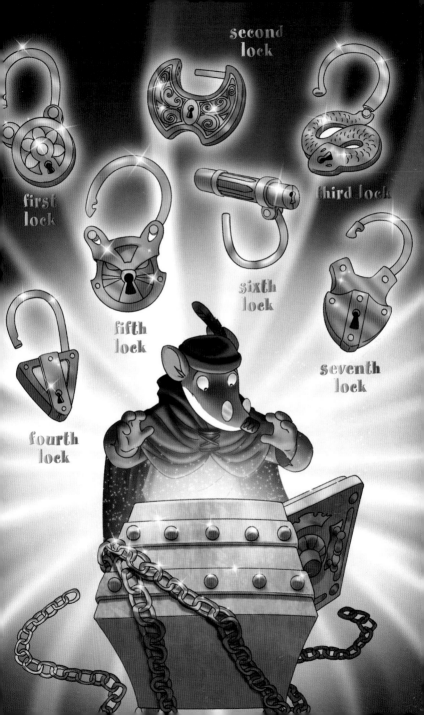

Cheese niblets, I was beyond excited! We had completed our mission! Now all we needed to do was escape from the witch's tower without being DISCOVERED and return to

CRYSTAL CASTLE

in time.

But when I reached out to grab the ring something happened I never expected. The safe bit me! That's right, Wither's crazy golden safe had **POINTY** teeth! It stared at me with EVIL EYES and then . . . Chomp!

Paws off, wise guy!

Ouchie!

That rotten safe bit my paw!

Before I could catch myself I yelled out at the top of my lungs, "Ouchie!"

At the same time the safe alerted the queen, screaming,

"HURRY, MY QUEEN, THE RING IS IN DANGER! THIEEEEFFFF!"

Wither woke up **IMMEDIATELY**. She was furious! Her eyes burned like embers. She grabbed her WAND and began shooting frightening flames!

As soon as she recovered from the shock, Wolfy held up her third magic wand.

She crossed wands with Wither and yelled out proudly, "En garde, witch! You don't scare me! I **CHALLENGE** you to a duel. Winner gets the ring!"

Wither shot Wolfy a, well, **WITHERING** look (what else?!). "You're making a mistake, a big

I will destroy you!

I'm not afraid!

mistake!" she screeched. "I will destroy you, you little wizard, and your little mouse, too!"

Wither **GATHERED** together her

DARK KNIGHTS

The Knights dragged us out of the castle and brought us to the **Buzz Buzz Swamp**.

"Okay, Miss Smarty Wizard" — Wither snickered — "I accept your **CHALLENGE**. We will have a

Magic Duel

And I will win!"

"It will be the **magic duel** of all times!" she continued. "It will be spoken about for years, no **FOREVER**, in the Kingdom of Fantasy!"

TAKE THAT!

Wolfy twirled around and transformed into a **WOLF**, gnashing her teeth. "I'm ready! Let's go!" she shouted.

Wither snickered. "Are you sure you're ready? Even to face the **dark fairies**?"

The fairies began to play their violins, **swirling** around Wolfy with their poisonous melody. Uh-oh. Wolfy called for backup.

In a **FLASH** Owlivia, Beartina, and Roxy appeared. "We're with you, Wolfy!" they yelled, quickly changing shape.

Owlivia stuck out her claws.

BEARTINA SWIPED WITH HER PAWS.

ROXY BARED HER TEETH.

Wither was furious. She called for her own backup.

THE MONSTERS OF THE FOUR DIRECTIONS!

Enormouse monsters of the north, east, south, and west arrived on the battlefield. They were scary monsters who used the power of **ICE**, **WIND**, **EARTH**, and **FIRE** as weapons.

To combat the monsters, Wolfy called the seven **VON WILD BROTHERS**. The brothers arrived and quickly transformed into dragon-headed knights.

The battle raged on and on . . .

Thunder!

lightning!

HAIL!

FOG!

Ice!

RAIN!

WIND!

The monsters and the seven Von Wild brothers
fought and fought and fought.

The magic battle lasted straight into the night. If only they had stopped for a **cheese** break. I was starving!

I was listening to my stomach grumble when Wither summoned **Stinkypus**.

BLISTERING BLUE CHEESE! Not that stinky beast.

Then Wolfy summoned LIGHTBRIGHT, THE DRAGON OF FORTUNE. He arrived in a shower of

And now I shall summon Stinkypus!

twinkling lights. He was pure magic!

The dragon and Stinkypus began to fight, blow for blow.

Meanwhile Stinkypus's terrible **stench** filled the air!

And I will call the Dragon of Fortune!

The stink of
Stinkypus

Stinkypus versus the
Dragon of Fortune

Still no one was defeated, so Wither called on

Toxic, the monster SCORPION with a thousand tails.

Toxic strutted onto the battlefield looking horrendous and frightening.

He shook his **poisonous** tail in the air. Then he reached out and stung Wolfy.

Luckily, before she fainted she summoned one more helper.

"I call on

UNITY,
the enchanted unicorn!"

Immediately, a magical WHITE UNICORN appeared. One touch from her golden horn and Wolfy was cured!

Wither ground her teeth in **ANGER** and stomped her foot.

I will cure you, Wolfy!

She yelled with a **thunderous** voice, "You think you're so smart, little wizard! You haven't seen anything yet! You asked for it!"

The witch waved her arm in the air and screeched, "Come forth, **GLOOM**, the shadow of sadness!" In a flash the battlefield was surrounded by a dense,

DARK SHADOW

that took away everyone's hope!

With the last of her **STRENGTH** Wolfy WHISPERED, "This is a job for the CLEVER CHAMELEON."

A moment later a strange lizard appeared wearing a robe. No, it wasn't a bathrobe. It was more like a robe you would wear to do karate. The lizard was small in size but he looked strong and calm. It was the Clever Chameleon. **GLOOM** had no **power** over him! He extended his hands and began to absorb Gloom's **dark** clouds and turn them into GOLDEN DUST...

Was it me? Or was this battle looking like it would never end?

Of course, it was Wither's turn next. She called on her

fiancé, Crowbar the Cruel, the Prince of Darkness.

An enormouse cloud made up of thousands and thousands of flying crows appeared. The crows were led by one crow that was **bigger** than the others and had FIERY eyes . . . it was CROWBAR THE CRUEL!

Still, before the crows could **_attack_**, Wolfy quickly pulled out her magic wand. She waved it in the air, summoning the powerful wind of the east.

With a whoosh, the wild eastern wind blew the birds away!

Wither and Wolfy called for reinforcements . . .

LIGHT IS MIGHT!

It seemed that every warrior from the *Kingdom of Fantasy* was getting in on the act. Just like Wither predicted, it was a battle to end all battles! Too bad it was **never-ending**!

I was considering proposing a **TIME-OUT** (who could object to a nap?) when Mel said, "I have an **IDEA**. Let's assemble the team of the

SECRET ALLIANCE.

Maybe together we can defeat the witches."

The Clever Chameleon, the Lady of Dreams, and Mel stood in a circle.

Mel gave me a crystal wand. "You will take Blossom's place, mouse," he instructed. "All you have to do is have **loving thoughts**."

I closed my eyes. Then I THOUGHT of all the *beautiful and good things in the world.*

We united our wands and yelled,

"Light is might!"

Zap!

The superstrong light made all the witches flee!

At that moment a SHIMMERING LIGHT illuminated the battlefield. It grew and grew until all of the witches grabbed their brooms and fled into the darkness.

Wither flew away, shrieking,

"MOUSE, I WILL GET MY REVENGE!"

Then she waved her wand at me one last time, and it shot out a flame. Luckily I jumped back just in time for the bolt to miss me! But then I noticed something else falling from her broom. It hit the ground with a

THUNK!

Cheese and crackers! It was the

Winged Ring!

I was so happy I did three cartwheels, a

backflip, and a split. Well, okay, I didn't really do GYMNASTICS, but you get the idea. I was thrilled!

Then Mel cleared his throat.

"Hold on, mouse," he said,

"You still

need to

complete

the

!"

THE RETURN TO CRYSTAL CASTLE

Where it is told of how Foolish One (finally) returned the Winged Ring to Blossom . . .

ARE YOU READY, FOOLISH ONE?

he wizard shot me a serious look. "Celebrate later. Let's wrap up this mission. Are you ready, Foolish One?"

I gulped. How could I wrap up the mission? "Um, well, I . . ." I stammered.

Are you ready?

Are you ready?

Umm . . . well, I . . .

I scratched my head. I was hoping returning the ring to Blossom would wrap up the mission. But apparently I was wrong. Oh, what would I have to do next? Climb a **treacherous** mountain? Fight a **FEROCIOUS** monster? Give up **cheese** for a week?

The Clever Chameleon tapped his cane on the ground. "Listen, mouse. You are either ready or you're not. Which is it?" he insisted.

Finally, Mel explained, "Night is almost over and the moon cycle is almost done! The gap between the two worlds must be closed by **dawn**! If you are late, Blossom will lose her **throne**!"

Oops! I had completely forgotten about the gap! Even though I had found the Winged Ring, I still hadn't completed my mission. But how do you close a gap between worlds?

Between sobs I asked, "But what can I do? I have no idea how to close a gap between worlds! Oh, what a disaster. I can't believe I messed everything up."

The Clever Chameleon **rolled** his eyes. "The gap can be fixed," he explained. "You just need two things: a needle and thread!"

Waaa!

It can be fixed . . .

Then he hit his cane on the ground and my tears, which made a kind of **puddle**, all concentrated together and formed one **LARGE CRYSTAL NEEDLE**.

I picked up the needle and examined it. It was TRANSPARENT. It was SHARP. And it was **HEAVY**.

A needle?

I took the *needle* and put it in my bag. Then I asked, "And where will I find the thread?"

The Lady of Dreams stepped forward. "To repair the gap created by Wither and the dark fairies you need a special thread! It must be . . . GOLDEN like a happy dream, *light* like air, and RESISTANT like eternal love!"

I blinked. Something told me borrowing some thread from my grandma Stitchy wouldn't do the trick. So I asked, "Where can I find the thread?"

"You must sing a song of love and harmony,"

said the Lady of Dreams. "The words that you sing will form the golden thread! Just be ready to grab the words with the needle before they *vanish* into thin air!"

The Lady of Dreams sang for me:

"Sing a song of love and joy,
And happiness that can't be destroyed.
Of all things good we hold so dear,
And words so light, and so sincere.
Each word will be a string of gold,
That ties the gap and keeps out the cold.
Words of kindness, true and strong,
To form gold thread ten miles long!"

I will remember all of it, thank you!

To be certain that I wouldn't forget, I wrote the words on a scroll.

Then Mel approached me and asked if I was ready to leave.

My heart began **hammering**. Oh, when would this **DANGEROUS** adventure finally come to an end? "Um, well, how do I get where I'm going?" I stammered.

"Not a problem," said Mel. "I will lend you

LIGHTBRIGHT, THE DRAGON OF FORTUNE!

When the Dragon of Fortune arrived I jumped on his back. Then I waved good-bye to Wolfy and all my friends.

"See you soon!" I called. I hoped I was right!

See you soon, friends!

DON'T THINK, JUST DO IT!

he Dragon of Fortune went higher . . .

and higher... and higher...

and higher... and higher...

and higher... and higher... and higher...

and higher... and higher...

and higher... and higher...

and higher... and higher...

toward the full moon glowing in the sky.

Puffy clouds drifted by in the inky night. And still the dragon continued to climb higher and higher and higher past *twinkling stars* as the moon grew bigger and bigger and bigger in the **cold, silvery light**.

Finally, the dragon stopped. The gap between the two worlds was right in front of us. My heart filled with sadness because all around I could hear the witches' *silver violins* . . .

This gap is enormouse!

The dragon suggested that I sit on the moon so I could sew in a nice ***bright light***. So I did.

"But **HURRY** with the sewing because I disappear at the first light of day! And if you're late, I won't have time to take you back to Blossom!" Lightbright warned.

So I positioned myself on the moon, took the

CRYSTAL NEEDLE

and, to make the thread, I remembered the words that the Lady of Dreams had told me. Then

I began to sing!

s good we

hold

so dear, And words so light and so sincere

Each word retells the story untold.

that ties the gap and keeps out cold.

the ember burning gold.

Words of kindness, true and dear

With that golden thread I began to fix the *tear* between the two worlds. The edges of the tear were **frayed**, and it wasn't easy to sew them together. Plus, I'm not the best at sewing. Or, er, to be completely honest, I am a terrible sewer! I once tried to sew a button on my jacket and ended up sewing it to my *tail* by accident! Ouch!

Still, there was no time to worry about my *sewing* skills. So I tried to remember what the Clever Chameleon had **advised**:

"Don't think, just do it!"

I concentrated on the words I was singing and ♥ the **love** in my heart. ♥ ♥ ♥

The **POiNt** of the needle went in . . . and came out . . . the thread brought the **frayed** edges closer together. I kept *sewing* for what seemed like forever, stitch after stitch . . . until finally, the entire gap was sewn. I had finished!

The gap between the two worlds was fixed! Only in that moment did I stop singing. No one would have guessed that that piece of the sky had been mended!

MY MISSION WAS COMPLETE!

CROWN ME!

I climbed aboard the Dragon of Fortune once more, and we flew at full speed toward Crystal Castle. The new day was about to **dawn** and the time to complete my mission was about to end! That's right, one moon cycle was almost done since I had left Crystal Castle. It seemed so much

LOOOOOOOOONGER!

Lightbright left me at Crystal Castle in that magical moment when the NIGHT isn't over and the day has not begun.

I entered the castle with my heart beating fast.

Now that I had the Winged Ring, would

Blossom go back to being the *queen*? Would the Fairies forgive me?

Maybe, maybe not... maybe, maybe not... maybe, maybe not... maybe, maybe not...

I opened the door to the throne room, looking for Blossom. But the throne was empty.

My friend was on her feet in the middle of all the

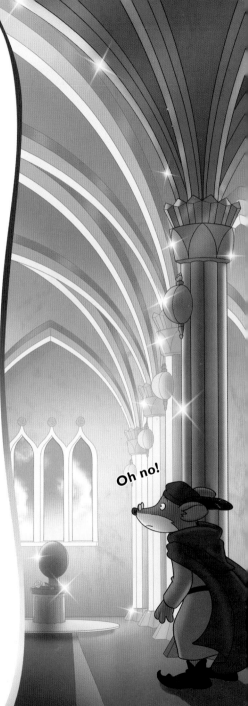

Oh no!

Crown me!

other fairies, just like any old fairy. And she didn't even have her **SPARKLING** crown on. Her **EYES** were filled with sadness. Oh no, Blossom wasn't queen anymore!

And it was all my fault...

Foolish One has returned!

Oh no!

The room was all ready to celebrate the coronation of a new king. In fact,

PRINCE WILLARD THE WEASELLY

had already moved his entire court in and brought everything for the ceremony to the castle!

The crowd muttered, "That's FOOLISH ONE, the one who lost the Winged Ring! Looks like he didn't find it. Now Blossom will be **EXILED.**"

WHAT ABOUT
THE PIZZAS?

ight then Willard ran up to me. He was already wearing a crown. Waving his scepter, he shrieked, "So, Foolish One, do you have the Winged Ring? Show it to us if you have it. *But you don't have it, ha, ha, haaa!* What are you waiting for?! Come on, I'm in a hurry to take my seat on the **THRONE**! Plus, I already prepared the celebratory banquet. Get moving, my **PIZZAS** are getting cold!"

Ignoring Willard, I turned to the fairies. "Fairy Court, I am here to return what was stolen from you, the Winged Ring!"

I slowly held out my paw. In it, the Winged Ring was SPARKLING!

The entire crowd YELLED out at once,

"OOOOOOHHHH!"

Blossom lifted her head, and I saw a glint of hope in her eyes.

With a JUMP, Willard approached me and tried to grab the ring, yelling hysterically, "No way! This isn't the Winged Ring. You can see quite clearly that it's a FAKE! Foolish One is lying. You can see that he's a liar! Don't fall for it! I am the new king of the Kingdom of Fantasy!

The throne is mine, mine, mine!"

But he was silenced by the oldest of the fairies, who turned to me. "Well, PRINCE, is it true what you say? Is this really the Winged Ring?"

I gave her the ring to inspect.

She examined it, then she **LIFTED** it in the air and proclaimed,

"The Winged Ring has been returned to crystal castle!"

The entire crowd cheered, "Hooray for Foolish One, the new hero of the Kingdom of Fantasy!"

It's the Winged Ring!

I blushed and muttered, "I'm no hero. I'm the one who **LOST** the ring in the first place."

When I looked up **JUDGE STRICTWINGS** was smiling at me.

She said, "Thanks, Foolish One. You have closed the **gap**

between Reality and Fantasy forever. You have repaired your mistake. The Fairy Court pardons you!"

Willard flipped his tail in anger. He grabbed the ring and **bit** into it to see if it was really fairy silver.

"Festering fur balls, it really is the ring!" he wailed. "And now I think I may have chipped my tooth!"

He pulled his whiskers in despair. "So then I won't be the king of the Kingdom of Fantasy! But what am I going to do with this gold crown? This can't be happening! Tell me I'm dreaming!"

His sister Willamena cried, "But . . . but . . . but . . . this means that I won't be the sister of the king, either! So what am I going to do with the *pen that's meant for signing important documents?*"

Then the two weasels sobbed together, "And what will we do with the printed invitations? And the pizzas for the coronation party! What will we do with the thirty-three thousand pizzas we ordered?"

Eventually the two left, consoling each other. "I guess we could use the crown as a flower stand. And we could use the silver scepter as a baseball bat," suggested one.

"And we could recycle the invitations and use them for our shopping lists for the next thirty years," said the other.

So many invitations . . .

Then they continued on, LiCKiNg their whiskers. "But what will

we do with the thirty-three thousand pizzas?"

"Well since we can't preserve them . . . we need to **EAT** them all ourselves!"

"Yum! Yum! And we even have a thousand of those F̈izzy tablets."

FIZZEROOS
Say good-bye to
INDIGESTION!

Your tummy helper, your Majesty!

Burp!

Yum! Yum! Yum!

Buuuurrrrpppp!

LONG LIVE THE QUEEN!

fter the weasels left, one of the fairies of the Fairy Court announced, "Let the Recrowning Ceremony begin! Once again, a Winged One, **Blossom of the Flowers**, will reign!"

Everyone clapped. Then **Blossom** stood up and the whole room grew *silent*. I mean, really silent. For instance, if I dropped a pin on the floor, the whole place would have heard it. Not that I had a pin on me. Why would I need a pin? Although, I did need that needle to *sew* up the gap between worlds . . .

Anyway, where was I? Oh yes, **Blossom** began to speak.

"My beloved subjects, today we have learned

many lessons. Foolish One has taught us a lesson about **FORGIVENESS** and loyalty. All of us mess up once in a while. So who are we to judge one another? When given the chance, Foolish One rose to the occasion and proved he is a most loyal friend to us all!

"And now I would like to thank you for crowning me *Queen of the Kingdom of Fantasy*. I will never take my job lightly. I love you all so very much!"

The crowd exploded in a cheer that made all the windows of Crystal Castle shake. "Long live the queen!"

The queen opened her arms, as if to **hug** all of the inhabitants of the Kingdom of Fantasy . . . fairies and elves, wizards, dwarves, and giants, gnomes and pixies, witches and warlocks, ogres, the greenies, the fruits and

Long live Blossom!

flowers and so many more. And a *feeling* of

PURE LOVE!

filled the room! Ah, what an amazing thing!

Then one by one we all pledged our loyalty to the queen.

Blue Rider took off his helmet and bowed before her. "I, Blue Rider, swear my loyalty to you!" he said.

Wolfy curtsied and said, "I, Wolfy, swear my loyalty to you!"

One after the other, all of her **old and new friends** lined up to swear their loyalty. She gave them all a **smile** that reached deep into their **hEARTS** as the crowd yelled,

"Long live the Winged Ones!"

kindness
harmony love wonder
tranquility
sweetness
loyalty
wonder
love ideal wonder light goodness
love happiness
wonder warmth positivity
light loyalty feeling
friendship harmony
friendship alliance peace serenity warmth friend
friend light tenderness positivity
goodness friend friendship harmony loyalty
tranquility feeling goodness light tenderness
kindness friendship feeling availability loyalty tenderness harmony serenity collaboration harmony
presence friend warmth tenderness generosity solidarity
sympathy light
well-being feeling kindness sweetness
attention sweetness gratitude care harmony
friendship goodness harmony warmth
friendship goodness
love understanding love friend friendship
positivity well-being
gratitude alliance kindness
happiness wonder ideal warmth trust
sisterhood
loyalty brotherhood
gratitude loving kindness care
feeling light tenderness presence friend love care
wonder warmth well-being
friend love care kindness friendship sweetness
affection trust
understanding warmth
solidarity
tenderness
union

What Should I Do?

inally, it was my turn. I put my paw over my heart and said, "Thank you for forgiving me, **Queen Blossom**."

She smiled. Then I asked, "Um, I was wondering . . . is there any way I can be called **Fearless, Prince of the Winged Ones**, again?"

Before she could respond, Mel **TAPPED** me

Hee, hee, hee!

It's not over yet!

Ouch!

on the head with his wand. "Did you really think it was that easy, Foolish One?" he asked. "You can't just get your title back the minute you give back the ring."

The Clever Chameleon nodded. "Yes, Foolish One," he agreed. "It is not that easy. Do you really feel you deserve the title FEARLESS ONE right now?"

I shook my head. "Uh, well, no actually. I have never been fearless. But a mouse can dream," I mumbled.

At this the Clever Chameleon chuckled. "Good! There is hope for you yet. I have straightened out many others worse off than you. I can straighten you out, too!"

Then he looked DEEPLY into my eyes, "Would you like to become a REAL HERO of the Kingdom of Fantasy? Someone who can always be counted on?" he asked.

I nodded so hard I accidentally bit my tongue. Ow!

"I wanth that from the bottom of my heARTh" I lisped.

The Clever Chameleon bowed his head. "Good, young student. Now follow me to my refuge on the BRIGHT MOUNTAINS. It is a place beyond the Kingdom of Fantasy, because it is outside of time and space. You will stay with me until you have learned."

I hesitated. "Umm, how much time will it take?"

He lifted his left eyebrow. "It will take a long time. Or a short time. *It all depends on you!*" he replied.

I gulped. I didn't want to insult the lizard, but I was missing my home squeak home. I stared at the ground. What should I do?

On the one paw I really wanted to follow

the Clever Chameleon and **LEARN** everything that I didn't know about becoming a **TRUE KNIGHT**. But when I thought about Mouse Island and my family, my heart *filled* with

longing.

TRY YOUR BEST!

I was still deciding what to do when Mel elbowed me in the side. "**MOUSE**, this is a great honor. If you don't accept, you really are a FOOL!" he muttered.

I nodded. Mel was right. I mean, how many times does a clever lizard ask you to go on an adventure with him?

"Okay, I have decided. I am coming with you, Clever Chameleon. Thank you for accepting me as your pupil," I replied.

Clev closed his eyes, satisfied. "From now on call me MASTER. Never interrupt me when I speak, do everything I say, and give everything you've got. Any questions?"

I chewed my whiskers. This adventure might be a lot harder than I thought. "I was

wondering," I said. "If I'm gone too long, I'm afraid my **FRIENDS** and **FAMILY** on Mouse Island will worry about me. Do you know how long this adventure will take?"

The lizard considered my question. Then he said, "*Time* does not exist in the Kingdom of Fantasy, so no one at your **home** will notice you are not there. As for the time it will take for your education, that all depends on you. I just expect you to do one thing:

Always try your best!"

At last it was time to leave. "We have a long, dangerous, scary, tiresome walk ahead of us!" said the chameleon.

WALK? I was exhausted already! I thought for sure we'd be taking a magical dragon or a

cloud balloon or something.

"Um, MASTER, do we have to walk?" I coughed.

"He who walks thinks like a hawk," the lizard replied.

Good-bye!

I had no idea what that meant. But it must have been something clever. After all, he was the CLEVER CHAMELEON!

When the lizard began walking I followed. Mel, Wolfy, and all of my other friends yelled, "Good-bye, Foolish One, see you soon!"

Let's go!

Have a good trip!

Good-bye, friends!

I waved. I hoped they were right about the "see you soon" part. I mean, don't get me wrong, traveling with the chameleon was exciting, but I would still miss my family, my COZY mouse bed, and my MEGA-HUGE FRIDGE filled with yummy cheese!

We walked for five hundred days and nights. All right, maybe it wasn't that long, but it sure felt like it! Eventually, we found ourselves at the bottom of a very tall mountain.

"Here's the Road of Light!" said the chameleon. "Here is the path we will climb to reach my Refuge! Come along now. We have a lot of work to do if you want to become a true FEARLESS knight!"

He walked up that steep path, and I followed. Of course, I was huffing and puffing. Hmmm . . . Maybe I could start an exercise program while I was at the refuge, too.

Meanwhile I thought of the incredible adventure that had just ended . . .

I had found the Winged Ring . . . The gap between the two worlds was closed . . .

Blossom was saved . . .

I did know one thing. I was ready! After all, if I never had any **EXCITING** adventures, I would have nothing to tell you, my dear readers.

I hope you liked this story.

I wrote it with love.

From your special mouse friend,

Geronimo Stilton!

The End

FANTASIAN ALPHABET

A	B	C	D	E
F	G	H	I	J
K	L	M	N	O
P	Q	R	S	T
U	V	W	X	Y	Z

0 1 2 3 4 5 6 7 8 9

Pages 10, 12–13, 14–15, 24

You see the shadow of an owl in the sky.

Pages 46–47

In the dragon costume.

Pages 52–53

The owl loses 11 feathers.

Pages 118–119

There are 37 gnomes.

Pages 130–131

Pages 64–65

ANSWERS

Pages 146–147
There are 8 squirrels.

Pages 150–151

Page 158
the mountain

Pages 160–161

Page 189
There are 36 names of trees.

Pages 190–191
There are 4 faces.

Pages 390–391

Pages 392–393
There are 20 lice.

Pages 274–275

ANSWERS

Pages 394–395
There are 10 vultures.

Pages 398–399
There are 8 trolls.

Pages 396–397

ANSWERS

Pages 408–409: There are 79 witches.

Pages 416–417

Pages 424–425

Pages 476–477

ABOUT THE AUTHOR

Born in New Mouse City, Mouse Island, **GERONIMO STILTON** is Rattus Emeritus of Mousomorphic Literature and of Neo-Ratonic Comparative Philosophy. For the past twenty years, he has been running *The Rodent's Gazette,* New Mouse City's most widely read daily newspaper.

Stilton was awarded the Ratitzer Prize for his scoops on *The Curse of the Cheese Pyramid* and *The Search for Sunken Treasure.* He has also received the Andersen 2000 Prize for Personality of the Year. One of his bestsellers won the 2002 eBook Award for world's best ratlings' electronic book. His works have been published all over the globe.

In his spare time, Mr. Stilton collects antique cheese rinds and plays golf. But what he most enjoys is telling stories to his nephew Benjamin.

Don't miss any of my adventures in the Kingdom of Fantasy!

THE KINGDOM OF FANTASY

THE QUEST FOR PARADISE:
THE RETURN TO THE KINGDOM OF FANTASY

THE AMAZING VOYAGE:
THE THIRD ADVENTURE IN THE KINGDOM OF FANTASY

THE DRAGON PROPHECY:
THE FOURTH ADVENTURE IN THE KINGDOM OF FANTASY

THE VOLCANO OF FIRE:
THE FIFTH ADVENTURE IN THE KINGDOM OF FANTASY

THE SEARCH FOR TREASURE:
THE SIXTH ADVENTURE IN THE KINGDOM OF FANTASY

THE ENCHANTED CHARMS:
THE SEVENTH ADVENTURE IN THE KINGDOM OF FANTASY

THE PHOENIX OF DESTINY:
AN EPIC KINGDOM OF FANTASY ADVENTURE

THE HOUR OF MAGIC:
THE EIGHTH ADVENTURE IN THE KINGDOM OF FANTASY

THE WIZARD'S WAND:
THE NINTH ADVENTURE IN THE KINGDOM OF FANTASY

THE SHIP OF SECRETS:
THE TENTH ADVENTURE IN THE KINGDOM OF FANTASY

THE DRAGON OF FORTUNE:
AN EPIC KINGDOM OF FANTASY ADVENTURE

Be sure to read all my fabumouse adventures!

#1 Lost Treasure of the Emerald Eye

#2 The Curse of the Cheese Pyramid

#3 Cat and Mouse in a Haunted House

#4 I'm Too Fond of My Fur!

#5 Four Mice Deep in the Jungle

#6 Paws Off, Cheddarface!

#7 Red Pizzas for a Blue Count

#8 Attack of the Bandit Cats

#9 A Fabumouse Vacation for Geronimo

#10 All Because of a Cup of Coffee

#11 It's Halloween, You 'Fraidy Mouse!

#12 Merry Christmas, Geronimo!

#13 The Phantom of the Subway

#14 The Temple of the Ruby of Fire

#15 The Mona Mousa Code

#16 A Cheese-Colored Camper

#17 Watch Your Whiskers, Stilton!

#18 Shipwreck on the Pirate Islands

#19 My Name Is Stilton, Geronimo Stilton

#20 Surf's Up, Geronimo!

#21 The Wild, Wild West

#22 The Secret of Cacklefur Castle

A Christmas Tale

#23 Valentine's Day Disaster

#24 Field Trip to Niagara Falls

#25 The Search for Sunken Treasure

#26 The Mummy with No Name

#27 The Christmas Toy Factory

#28 Wedding Crasher

#29 Down and Out Down Under

#30 The Mouse Island Marathon

#31 The Mysterious Cheese Thief

Christmas Catastrophe

#32 Valley of the Giant Skeletons

#33 Geronimo and the Gold Medal Mystery

#34 Geronimo Stilton, Secret Agent

#35 A Very Merry Christmas

#36 Geronimo's Valentine

#37 The Race Across America

#38 A Fabumouse School Adventure

#39 Singing Sensation

#40 The Karate Mouse

#41 Mighty Mount Kilimanjaro

#42 The Peculiar Pumpkin Thief

#43 I'm Not a Supermouse!

#44 The Giant Diamond Robbery

#45 Save the White Whale!

#46 The Haunted Castle

Geronimo Stilton

#47 Run for the Hills, Geronimo!

#48 The Mystery in Venice

#49 The Way of the Samurai

#50 This Hotel Is Haunted!

#51 The Enormouse Pearl Heist

#52 Mouse in Space!

#53 Rumble in the Jungle

#54 Get into Gear, Stilton!

#55 The Golden Statue Plot

#56 Flight of the Red Bandit

Special Edition! The Hunt for the Golden Book

#57 The Stinky Cheese Vacation

#58 The Super Chef Contest

#59 Welcome to Moldy Manor

Special Edition! The Hunt for the Curious Cheese

#60 The Treasure of Easter Island

#61 Mouse House Hunter

#62 Mouse Overboard!

Special Edition! The Hunt for the Secret Papyrus

#63 The Cheese Experiment

#64 Magical Mission

#65 Bollywood Burglary

Special Edition! The Hunt for the Hundredth Key

#66 Operation: Secret Recipe

#67 The Chocolate Chase

Meet
GERONIMO STILTONOOT

He is a cavemouse — Geronimo Stilton's ancient ancestor! He runs the stone newspaper in the prehistoric village of Old Mouse City. From dealing with dinosaurs to dodging meteorites, his life in the Stone Age is full of adventure!

#1 The Stone of Fire

#2 Watch Your Tail!

#3 Help, I'm in Hot Lava!

#4 The Fast and the Frozen

#5 The Great Mouse Race

#6 Don't Wake the Dinosaur!

#7 I'm a Scaredy-Mouse!

#8 Surfing for Secrets

#9 Get the Scoop, Geronimo!

#10 My Autosaurus Will Win!

#11 Sea Monster Surprise

#12 Paws Off the Pearl!

#13 The Smelly Search

#14 Shoo, Caveflies!

#15 A Mammoth Mystery

MEET GERONIMO STILTONIX

He is a spacemouse — the Geronimo Stilton of a parallel universe! He is captain of the spaceship *MouseStar 1*. While flying through the cosmos, he visits distant planets and meets crazy aliens. His adventures are out of this world!

#1 Alien Escape

#2 You're Mine, Captain!

#3 Ice Planet Adventure

#4 The Galactic Goal

#5 Rescue Rebellion

#6 The Underwater Planet

#7 Beware! Space Junk!

#8 Away in a Star Sled

#9 Slurp Monster Showdown

#10 Pirate Spacecat Attack

#11 We'll Bite Your Tail, Geronimo!

Don't miss any of these exciting Thea Sisters adventures!

Thea Stilton and the
Dragon's Code

Thea Stilton and the
Mountain of Fire

Thea Stilton and the
Ghost of the Shipwreck

Thea Stilton and the
Secret City

Thea Stilton and the
Mystery in Paris

Thea Stilton and the
Cherry Blossom Adventure

Thea Stilton and the
Star Castaways

Thea Stilton: Big Trouble
in the Big Apple

Thea Stilton and the
Ice Treasure

Thea Stilton and the
Secret of the Old Castle

Thea Stilton and the
Blue Scarab Hunt

Thea Stilton and the
Prince's Emerald

Thea Stilton and the
Mystery on the Orient Express

Thea Stilton and the
Dancing Shadows

Thea Stilton and the
Legend of the Fire Flowers

Thea Stilton and the
Spanish Dance Mission

Thea Stilton and the
Journey to the Lion's Den

**Thea Stilton and the
Great Tulip Heist**

**Thea Stilton and the
Chocolate Sabotage**

**Thea Stilton and the
Missing Myth**

**Thea Stilton and the
Lost Letters**

**Thea Stilton and the
Tropical Treasure**

**Thea Stilton and the
Hollywood Hoax**

**Thea Stilton and the
Madagascar Madness**

**Thea Stilton and the
Frozen Fiasco**

**Thea Stilton and the
Venice Masquerade**

And check out my fabumouse special editions!

**THEA STILTON:
THE JOURNEY
TO ATLANTIS**

**THEA STILTON:
THE SECRET OF
THE FAIRIES**

**THEA STILTON:
THE SECRET OF
THE SNOW**

**THEA STILTON:
THE CLOUD
CASTLE**

**THEA STILTON:
THE TREASURE
OF THE SEA**

**THEA STILTON:
THE LAND OF
FLOWERS**

Meet
CREEPELLA VON CACKLEFU

I, *Geronimo Stilton*, have a lot of mouse friends, but none as **spooky** as my friend CREEPELLA VON CACKLEFUR! She is an enchanting and MYSTERIOUS mouse with a pet bat named Bitewing. YIKES! I'm a real 'fraidy mouse, but even I think CREEPELLA and her family are AWFULLY fascinating. I can't wait for you to read all about CREEPELLA in these fa-mouse-ly funny and **spectacularly spooky** tales!

#1 The Thirteen Ghosts   **#2 Meet Me in Horrorwood**   **#3 Ghost Pirate Treasure**   **#4 Return of the Vampire**   **#5 Fri**

#6 Ride for Your Life!   **#7 A Suitcase Full of Ghosts**   **#8 The Phantom of the Theater**   **#9 The Haunted Dinosaur**

MEET
Geronimo Stiltonord

He is a mouseking — the Geronimo Stilton of the ancient far north! He lives with his brawny and brave clan in the village of Mouseborg. From sailing frozen waters to facing fiery dragons, every day is an adventure for the micekings!

#1 Attack of the Dragons

#2 The Famouse Fjord Race

#3 Pull the Dragon's Tooth!

#4 Stay Strong, Geronimo!

#5 The Mysterious Message

#6 The Helmet Holdup

THE JOURNEY THROUGH TIME

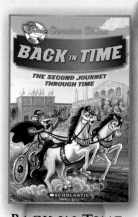

BACK IN TIME:
THE SECOND JOURNEY THROUGH TIME

THE RACE AGAINST TIME:
THE THIRD JOURNEY THROUGH TIME

LOST IN TIME:
THE FOURTH JOURNEY THROUGH TIME

Dear rodent
friends . . .

. . . good-bye until the next journey to the Kingdom of Fantasy!